An
famuy in the suburbs of Dublin, Ireland. Her love of
romance was inspired after
mother's beloved Mills & F
twelve. Writing soon becan
her wildly overactive imagi
a daughter of her own, she
changing nappies, studying
love stories.

CLAIMING HIS REPLACEMENT QUEEN

AMANDA CINELLI

MILLS & BOON

First Published in Great Britain 2019
by Mills & Boon, an imprint of HarperCollins*Publishers*
1 London Bridge Street, London, SE1 9GF

© 2019 Amanda Cinelli

ISBN: 978-0-263-27070-9

MIX
Paper from
responsible sources
FSC˚ C007454

This book is produced from independently certified FSC™ paper
to ensure responsible forest management.
For more information visit www.harpercollins.co.uk/green.

Printed and bound in Spain
by CPI, Barcelona

For Emily

CHAPTER ONE

'*I'D RATHER DIE than be your wife a moment longer.*'

Khal opened his eyes, clean cool air filling his lungs with painful force. His surroundings were a jolt to his system, the sleek interior of the royal jet's main cabin so far apart from the angry red sands and fathomless black water of his dream. It had just been a dream. He sat back, looking up at the ceiling as his heartbeat found its rhythm once more.

His subconscious had long ago stopped tormenting him with every detail of his last conversation with his wife before her death. Or so he had believed.

He unbuckled his seat belt and stood, stretching out the painful tightness in his shoulders. He could have chosen to sleep in any one of the three luxurious bedrooms on board, but sleep had not come easily of late. The dreams were back with a vengeance. The same dreams that had plagued him for an entire year after his wife's death. Stress seemed to be a trigger and the past few weeks had most certainly not been a relaxing time.

He pressed a button on the panel by his side and, as if by magic, two flight attendants emerged from the end of the cabin. A tray bearing hot towels and fresh ice water was placed on the nearest table without a word.

His chair was returned to the upright position and a pot of hot coffee set down within reach.

'That will be all, thank you,' he said, his voice unintentionally gravelly from sleep. He glanced up just in time to see one of the women visibly flinch as he waved one hand in dismissal. He fought the urge to roll his eyes with irritation. Without another word, they hurried back behind the curtain and he was alone once more. Just as he preferred it.

Most of his staff knew him well enough to disregard the rumours that had spread upon his wife's untimely passing. Disgusting, slanderous rumours that he had worked hard to dispel even while in the first days of his grief. But still, whispers spread and somehow the idea that he was a man to be feared had stuck.

People believed him to be a villain and it suited him to keep it that way. He was not forced to make idle conversation, to pretend to care. He did not throw social functions nor did he attend a great many.

Or at least he hadn't until recently.

Khal opened his laptop and scanned an assortment of international news articles that his press team had collated from the past week. *The Most Romantic Royal Love Story of the Decade*, one headline proclaimed. It was any news reporter's dream, Princess Olivia of the tiny European kingdom of Monteverre turning her back on her lofty title to marry a man her family deemed unsuitable. One picture showed Khal's close friend Roman Lazarov as he walked hand in hand with the beautiful redhead. What a cruel twist of fate it was that the woman he had finally chosen as his second wife, the answer to all his economic woes, would be snatched up at the last moment. And by his best friend, no less.

Remarrying had never been in his plans for his reign as Sheikh. He had been a young man on his first wedding day, filled with naïve hope for the future. That version of himself was long gone. He had no desire to find a woman to mend his broken heart, or any of the other schemes he had heard whispered by his mother and sister when they thought he could not hear. Thanks to his sister, he had two strong nephews that would carry on the Al Rhas bloodline and therefore he'd believed he had absolutely no need for a wife.

But he could no longer deny that the rumours surrounding his wife's demise were affecting Zayyar's international image. His country had been peaceful for over two decades, his father and grandfather before him credited with having brought their small Middle Eastern kingdom back from the brink of complete ruin. Khal had no wish for fame or a place in the history books, but he refused to be remembered as the Sheikh who had ruined all of their hard work.

Known for his careful planning, he had spent months drawing up an arrangement with Monteverre, one of the oldest and most financially troubled kingdoms in Europe. It was a deal that would solve all his problems in one fell swoop. He would provide the Monteverrian economy with a very healthy injection of capital and in return he would gain a loyal alliance in the form of the perfect bride with the perfect amount of political influence and public appeal.

By now the whole world knew that the Princess had given up her formal title to be with her scandalous Russian lover. There was no mention of a failed engagement to the Sheikh of Zayyar in any newspaper, nor would there ever be, thanks to his team. His name rarely graced any of the world media sources, nor did paparazzi images. He paid handsomely for his privacy. And a good thing too, considering he was about to arrive unannounced into a foreign country to retrieve his replacement bride.

He knew nothing of the youngest Sandoval Princess, only that she had been studying abroad in England for many years and had agreed to his offer of a royal marriage of convenience with very little hesitation. She had even agreed to sign a formal engagement contract without first meeting in person. He should feel relieved that his plans had not been completely derailed, and yet something seemed off.

He had amended the terms of the agreement from its original form, limiting the deal to five years of marriage in name only, followed by an easy divorce settlement. With such a solid link to European royalty provided by his bride, five years would be more than enough time for him to repair the bridges that had been burned by his reputation. Divorce was a common occurrence across the globe; Zayyar was no different. Still, he knew he would not truly rest until he had spoken to his fiancée in person.

He spent the remainder of the flight in quiet contemplation, barely noticing that they had landed until his pilot announced the incredibly low temperature in the city of London. It was the middle of May and yet he felt the need to pull up the collar of his impeccably tailored wool coat as he made the short trip from jet to limousine, grateful that he had chosen to change into Western-style clothing mid-flight. His usual flowing white robes were perfect for the desert heat, but not designed for the chilly, wet weather so common in this part of the world.

His Chief of Security sat waiting in the car, his expression stressed—Sayyid never looked stressed. Immediately Khal's instincts stood to attention.

'There has been a small problem,' Sayyid said solemnly.

Khal kept his features expressionless as his trusted servant outlined the events of the past twenty-four hours' surveillance operation. Finally, he closed his eyes, fighting the urge not to slam his fist into the door panel. 'You believe she is a flight risk?'

'She shows all of the signs of it, Sire.' After a prolonged silence, Sayyid cleared his throat quietly. 'If you give me the order, I will have the Princess collected immediately and delivered to the jet.'

'Your men are currently in pursuit?' Khal spoke with quiet control, hardly believing history was repeating itself so blatantly.

'She is safely surrounded and unaware of their presence.'

Khal nodded, running a hand across the light stubble on his jaw. He had already taken King Fabian's word once and been burned, but this time it was different. He had sent his personal secretary to London with official documents and ensured that Her Highness signed them herself in person. He had done everything within his power to ensure her complete consent before entering into a legally binding engagement to protect his investment. If she walked away from their engagement now, the repercussions for her kingdom were grave.

Surely she realised that?

But of course he had to be prepared for the fact that

maybe she did not care. Nonetheless, at this moment in time she was his fiancée. And in Zayyar that was as good as already being his wife. He had a duty to ensure her safety. Princess Cressida might be having second thoughts about their marriage, but he'd be damned if he would send anyone in to talk her round this time, other than himself.

'I'll handle this myself.' He spoke with a calm he did not feel. 'Take me to her.'

The exclusive club was a secret to most Londoners, hidden away behind the rather nondescript black door of a Georgian townhouse in Mayfair. The chilly breeze brushed across her skin as Cressida Sandoval stepped out onto the pavement and looked up at the building's dimly lit facade. The urge to abandon her plans and retreat to the warm interior of the limousine was strong. Frank, her loyal chauffeur of five years, was not happy with her insistence that he remain behind and he'd made his disapproval known by slamming the door audibly behind her.

'Your Highness, are you sure you don't want me to escort you inside?' He spoke quietly, worrying his black tie with one hand.

Cressida stiffened at the honorific. The title that set her so far apart from every other twenty-four-year-old woman seeking a night of freedom. She inhaled softly, reminding herself that her freedom relied entirely on the driver's discretion. 'I have never asked for a favour before now.'

He shook his head, leaning back against the car bonnet. 'Five years of driving you from home to Oxford,

Oxford to home, like blimmin' clockwork. Last night on the job and you've decided to give me heart failure.'

'Two hours alone, Frank. That's all I want.' She understood his worry; his job would be on the line if anything happened to her on his watch. If she'd had any street sense she would probably have taken a cab, but princesses did not take cabs, nor did they sneak out unaccompanied to secret clubs in the dead of night. She'd had to dodge her two bodyguards and beg Frank, just to get him to agree to drive her and wait outside. Once the time was up, she would return to reality. Or at least the suffocating reality of what her life had recently become.

Her father's voice rang in her ears.

'Politically advantageous...royal duty...for the good of the kingdom.'

Tomorrow she would become Princess Cressida Sandoval once more, returning to her kingdom after five years of self-imposed exile. Her father, the King of Monteverre, had barely listened to her weak argument about the European languages doctorate she had signed up for or the assistant teaching position she had been offered. 'Princesses do not *teach*, Cressida,' he had boomed in his usual way. 'I'm sure the Sheikh will have plenty of dusty old books for you to bury your nose in, or whatever it is that you've been wasting your time with for the past five years.'

The Sheikh. Her future husband.

She should not feel so nervous about something that was essentially just a business arrangement. Five years of service, her father had said. How utterly romantic. Not that romance had ever played a part in her life so far, but still... She had been comfortable here in London, away from the watching eyes of the public. Was she truly ready to become a queen?

A fresh wave of anxiety fuelled her with adrenaline as she met the eyes of the burly man guarding the door to the club. She quietly spoke the code word she had overheard three nights before from one of her bodyguards. The door was opened without comment, revealing plush red carpeted stairs with sleek chrome handrails descending downwards. She paused for a moment, fear of the unknown snaking around her chest and pulling tight. The low hum of music and conversation drifted upwards like a siren's song.

This was her last night in London, she reminded herself as she took the first step downwards. She owed it to herself to experience at least a taste of the freedom she had stupidly taken for granted before her face graced the front of every newspaper on the globe.

She had felt the walls closing in on her as she'd signed her name on each document that had been presented to her, precious control slipping through her fingers. Perhaps that was why she was acting on impulse for the first time in her life. She was overcome with the need to go somewhere new and be someone anonymous for just a few short hours before doing The Right Thing.

Because, when it came to royal duty, she always did what was asked of her. Whether she liked it or not.

She had felt on edge from the moment she'd ended that fateful phone call with her father. Knowing that she would do as he asked, even if it was not what she wanted. He knew it too. He knew that she always felt the pressure to measure up to her older sisters. It was so much more than simple sibling rivalry. He had always made it clear that she was his least favourite, the daughter he simply tolerated. Her thoughts turned dark, thinking of that fateful day when, as a twelve-year-old, she had finally found out why...

Pausing at the end of the stairway, Cressida took in the image of a sultry blonde in red and took a deep breath as she realised it was her own reflection. Her dark blonde locks fell in soft waves around her face, free from their usual tight ponytail. Her plain black glasses had been replaced by contact lenses. Her jeans and sneakers gone, in favour of a stylish red dress and heels slightly too high for comfort. She had devoted more time and research to tonight's outfit than she'd given to her most recent thesis. She was good at research. It was the practical application that made her insides shake. But suddenly, standing looking at this strange, almost pretty version of herself, the bands around her chest loosened a little and she felt a hint of that freedom she so craved.

The club was deceptively spacious inside, much larger than it seemed from the narrow building facade. The décor was a modern monochrome with a hint of old world glamour in the large sparkling chandeliers that hung from the ceiling at various points. A small stage with a live jazz band dominated one corner of the large space while a double-sided bar with floor-to-ceiling mirrors glittered in the middle. It was like walking into an old black-and-white movie.

Cressida walked towards the bar as confidently as she could muster, ignoring the painful beat of her heart high up in her throat.

The music was fast paced but sensual, accentuated by a husky-toned singer in a scandalously short dress and elbow-length gloves. As she slid onto a bar stool she spied a line of strategically roped-off areas towards the back, some filled with very beautiful but rather bored-looking people. The nameless secret basement club was known for its A-list clientele and its air of anonymity, according to the conversation she had overheard between her two bodyguards. No paparazzi allowed.

Even though it was a weeknight, the club was filled with people dancing and moving to the music as the lighting curved around them. As she looked on, a famous blonde singer stood up on a table and began to pour a bottle of expensive-looking champagne over the people around her. The group of men and women began dancing and gyrating under the spray, laughing and singing along to the music.

She found herself smiling in wonder at the sight of such ridiculous behaviour. If she were to truly enjoy her freedom, she would just stand and join in with the dancing and no one would look twice at her... The thought came and passed as she took a seat at the end of the long bar, comfortably on the outskirts of the action.

Soon she would probably need to ask for permission before doing something so daring as dancing in public; she felt her mouth curve downwards.

She could refuse the match, of course. This was not some medieval drama where she would be bound and dragged down the aisle, whether she agreed to the union or not. She adored the simple life she had begun to carve out for herself here in London but of course she knew it was not allowed for a member of royalty to take a paid job. She was not meant for such blissful normality as being a teaching assistant, much as she had been delighted to be offered the position. She had a duty to ·erve the people of Monteverre.

She ordered a white wine, not feeling confident enough to order anything else. She occasionally drank a glass with dinner, but never more. Alcohol dulled her senses in a way that simply did not appeal to her orderly nature. She sipped slowly, feeling slightly at sea amidst the raucous dancing and groupings of people. Mingling had never been a forte of hers. The word itself made her feel twitchy. She remembered herself as a young girl, wishing she was more confident, more natural at being a princess. She had always felt so different to her older sisters, the stereotypical mousy wallflower to their flame-haired beauty. And then one day everything had changed and she had simply stopped trying. She had found comfort in blending into the background where it was safer, where no one looked too closely at her...

You came here to feel free and here you are, hiding in the corner feeling sorry for yourself. She bit her lip hard, swirling the golden liquid in her glass and watching the light play on the surface. She became suddenly aware of a shadow in the reflection of the glass and the delicious scent of a warm, distinctly male cologne.

She looked up.

Goodness...

Tall, dark and handsome simply did not describe the man standing a mere foot away from her. This man was broad, exotic and breathtaking. She swallowed hard as dark, hooded eyes met hers. He didn't make a move to speak and after a long moment her awkward nature interfered, her voice trembling slightly as she asked, 'Can I help you?'

His expression changed fleetingly to one of mild surprise, making her wonder if he had mistaken her for someone else. His gaze moved down to take in he long legs crossed on the high barstool before returning to her face. She half hoped he had made a mistake, then perhaps he would leave and she might be able to breathe normally again.

'Are you expecting someone?' He gestured to the empty barstool beside her. His voice was a deep accented rumble.

'No. I'm here alone,' she said quickly, then worried if that made her seem a little bit needy. 'I mean, the seat is yours. If you want it, that is. It's…not mine, either way.' She felt her cheeks heat. She was a babbling idiot.

A tension-filled silence followed and the stranger's eyes narrowed slightly as though he were waiting for her to say something more. A strange bewildered expression crossed his face as he moved to sit back onto a barstool, leaving the seat between them empty.

Cressida frowned, one hand idly tracing the edge of her glass as she shot a sidelong glance towards the mysterious hunk. Nipping at her bottom lip with her teeth, she took a slow sip of her wine to cool her suddenly dry throat. He was handsome, there was no denying it, with warm mahogany-toned skin and jet black stubble shadowing his jawline.

The shadow that began on his jawline continued down a strong throat to disappear into the open collar of a perfect white shirt. A white shirt that covered the broadest shoulders she had ever seen…

She moved her gaze back up to find a pair of dark eyes watching her. Startled, she inhaled sharply and promptly breathed in a mouthful of wine. Her throat convulsed in a series of loud embarrassing coughs and she was vaguely aware of a napkin appearing in her peripheral vision. She prayed her eye make-up hadn't run and silently willed the dark stranger to disappear so that she didn't have to continue her embarrassment any longer.

She froze as he placed a glass of water into her hands, the heat of his fingers scorching her skin for a few short seconds. The cold water calmed both her raw throat and her overheated brain.

Cressida looked up to find he had moved to the seat directly beside her. This close, she could see tiny flecks of gold in his deep brown irises. The way he was looking at her so intently made her feel as though she had walked under a spotlight. She was too warm, too exposed.

'Thank you,' she blurted, forcing herself to meet his eyes. 'For the water.'

'It's my pleasure.' His eyes did not leave hers. 'However, I believe it is now irresponsible of me to leave you unsupervised while you finish your drink.'

'I must seem quite ridiculous, really.' Cressida half laughed, feeling rather blinded under the intense spotlight of his attention.

'That's the last word I would use,' he said silkily, tilting his head to one side.

She managed a slight smile, wondering again why he had chosen to sit with her. Men like him did not show interest in women like her; it was hard not to be suspicious. Not that she was here seeking male attention; far from it. Tonight was simply about freedom, she reminded herself with a firm shrug of her shoulders.

'I find myself wondering…' his dark voice rumbled somewhere close to her ear '…what might have brought you here tonight to this particular club?'

Cressida felt the vibration of his deep voice trave

down to her toes. She shifted in her seat. 'The same reason as everyone else, I assume. It's an escape.'

'You are looking to escape something?'

'If I say the outside world, is that rather a cliché?'
She grimaced with a half laugh, feeling herself relax
slightly. 'I must go back eventually, of course.'

He seemed thoughtful for a moment. 'While you are
here, what do you plan to do?'

'I hadn't really thought that far ahead.' She laughed,
shocked at how feminine she sounded. 'I'm trying to be
spontaneous for once. Perhaps I might dance?'

'Alone?'

'If no one asked me, I suppose I would have to dance
alone.' It was hardly a suggestive statement, but still
she felt herself blush a little, knowing she suddenly
wanted him to ask her to dance. What on earth had
come over her?

She had never flirted with a man before—she wasn't
even sure if this qualified as flirting—but it definitely
felt different to any previous conversations with a member of the opposite sex. What was she even doing? She
was promised to another man, both morally and legally.
She might not have met her fiancé yet, but she still knew
where the boundaries stood. But a simple dance…that
was hardly improper. Maybe it was the wine, though
she knew herself that two sips could hardly provide
enough stimulant. It was becoming intoxicating, feeling so free. That was the only explanation. It was making her feel different, bolder.

'By all means, then. You should dance,' he said.

'Yes, I would love to.' She smiled, feeling the sense
of bravado heighten further. She slid off the barstool,
biting her lower lip as he made no move to stand.

You should dance, he had said, not *we*. Silly girl.

She smiled a little too widely before turning to take a few steps towards the crowded dance floor. Throwing a final look over her shoulder as she walked away, she found herself momentarily pinned by a dark gaze. Heat sizzled through the air, seeming to settle somewhere in the region of her solar plexus.

Her painfully shy nature and workaholic tendencies had stopped her from ever having a dating life. So much so that the opposite sex might well have become a foreign species altogether, apart from her interactions with her bodyguards and driver. She could read and write fluently in eight languages and yet she could not formulate a simple sentence in English to ask a man if he wanted to dance with her. It was so utterly ridiculous that she laughed. Her laughter caught the attention of a blond-haired man nearby and he moved to dance beside her.

She smiled back briefly and continued dancing, distracted by wondering if *he* was still sitting at the bar, watching her. It was a ridiculous thought, that a complete stranger might feel the same hum of attraction after a moment of idle conversation. It was not as though she planned to do anything about it, but she had to admit it felt nice being noticed.

In the background, she registered the beat shifting seamlessly into a soft, seductive ballad. She let her gaze drift around the dance floor just as a handful of couples moved close and began moulding their bodies together sensually. She looked away for a moment then looked back, transfixed by the sight of a couple melting together in a haze of locked lips and intertwined limbs all the while maintaining a perfect rhythm.

Without warning, the blond man moved close. A chunky arm snaked around her waist and she froze. She took a step away, trying to think of a kind way to decline the dance without hurting his feelings, but he moved with her, not forcefully but still determined to get close. Needing to be free of the situation, she placed her hand calmly against the man's chest, shaking her head to show that she was leaving. Worried he wasn't going to take the hint, she turned fully and took a few steps away from the dance floor, only to be blocked by a wall of warm, hard muscle.

'Waiting for me?' The stranger's deep voice was like a balm to her nerves as he extended a hand towards her. To her surprise, she instantly placed her hand in his, allowing herself to be drawn into the delicious warm scent of his cologne until their bodies were mere inches apart. She was vaguely aware of the other man disappearing into the crowd, but it was becoming increasingly harder to form a coherent thought as a strong male arm moved slowly around her waist.

The smooth, steady rhythm of the music seemed to pound through the wall of her chest before joining her own erratic heartbeat. He pulled her close. So close that the smooth dark skin of his open collar was directly in her eye line, mere inches away. The tips of her breasts pressed momentarily against a wall of warm hard muscle before he moved back slightly. Her free hand hovered uncertainly for a moment before she bravely moved it upwards to link around his neck, her fingers resting between warm skin and the thick dark hair of his nape as he led her into an easy rhythm.

She had been given the finest dancing lessons as a young teenager to prepare her for the many occasions that a princess was required to perform a simple waltz or foxtrot. Nine times out of ten she tripped over her own feet, of course, but she knew the basics. But none of that could have prepared her for this moment. They seemed to dance for hours, moving in perfect unison. He was an excellent lead, confident and strong. He held her in such a way that she almost felt graceful for the first time in her life. His hands did not wander from their place on her waist; he didn't even try to pull her too close against him. She felt safe, she realised. What a strange thing to feel in the arms of a man she barely knew.

Her dark stranger bent his head and for a moment she wondered if he planned to kiss her. She held her breath, relaxing when instead his mouth stopped somewhere just above her earlobe.

'In my country, dancing like this is considered a very intimate act.' His voice was a soft rumble that sent an earthquake of shivers down her spine.

'Is that so?' Cressida breathed, hardly believing that such a husky murmur had just escaped her own suddenly dry throat. 'I can't imagine why.'

A mischievous smile played on his lips. 'You can't?'

'People dance all of the time. It's hardly dangerous.'

'I'm not so sure,' he murmured. 'Swaying like this… pressed so close… I can see how it would be seen as temptation.'

'Temptation for what…?' Her feverish brain wondered momentarily at his choice of words before realisation dawned with all the grace of a sledgehammer. She clumsily missed a step but her dancing partner barely reacted, correcting her misstep with graceful ease and continuing as though nothing had occurred.

'It is usually only married couples who might dance like this,' he continued, oblivious to her embarrassment. 'Or perhaps those who are engaged to be married.'

She barely registered his words as her mind focused on the heat of his hand as it began to move higher on her waist, resting ever so slightly on the bared skin of her lower back. It was as though the movement of his hand shifted some kind of invisible barrier between them. She looked up, meeting the visible heat in his eyes for a long silent moment. The air seemed to pulse with heat along with the slow seductive crooning of the jazz in the background.

Suddenly it felt as though every inch of her front was glued to a wall of warm hard muscle. Her body felt heated and loose in his arms, her mind telling her to move closer. A tiny fragment of her logical brain warned her to walk away. She ignored it.

'I doubt anyone else in here considers slow dancing to be such an important act.' She kept her tone even, trying to maintain some level of worldly composure in the face of her body's ridiculous reaction.

'I had quite forgotten that there was anyone else here at all,' he said softly.

Cressida looked up to meet his eyes; they were dark and earnest, no trace of humour or sarcasm. She felt her cheeks heat, her eyes lowering to rest comfortably on his chin. This was it, she told herself sternly—this was the moment where she should thank him for a lovely dance and make a calm and graceful exit.

The dance had been perfect, she told herself sternly—exactly what she had needed. She had sought a little excitement on her night of freedom and now she would leave London tomorrow and go happily to her duty. She could forget about this night, forget about this handsome stranger and easily go on for ever without wondering...

Suddenly she became aware that they had stopped dancing. The music had got faster and the other couples moved around the spot where they stood, entirely still in their embrace. She looked up. He was still watching her with that impenetrable gaze in a moment that seemed to stretch on as though separate from time entirely. His fingers flexed slightly at her waist, sending tingles up her spine.

What would it be like to feel his mouth on hers and his hands roaming over her body? The thought caught her by surprise, her cheeks heating as she ran the tip of her tongue along her suddenly dry lips. Her sister had described a kind of madness that had taken over when she'd met the man who was now her fiancé, an attraction that had overcome logic and reason. She doubted she could ever harbour such a passion. All of a sudden she despised the calm, rational Cressida who lived in fear of straying too far from her comfort zone. What would it feel like to simply have a thought pop into one's mind and act on it? To be a different version of herself, even for just a moment?

He cleared his throat and she felt the moment slipping away; the small window of time she had been granted seemed to be disappearing, leaving nothing but the promise of tomorrow. Of the life being forced upon her. The choices she would no longer be free to make. *But not yet...*a small voice inside whispered.

She looked up into the deep brown of his gaze, catching her breath at the blatant heat she saw there. Madness indeed, she thought as her breath stopped completely, realising what she was about to do. Letting impulse take the lead, she flexed her body upwards and pressed her lips to his.

Soft, firm lips remained still under the clumsy touch of her inexperienced kiss. The hands on her waist applied pressure, holding her where she stood as his lips began to move against hers, hard and fast. Suddenly the kiss was demanding and filled with a hunger that took her breath away. It was intoxicating and overwhelming and…utterly perfect.

Was this what everyone felt when they kissed a man for the first time? Was this what she had been missing out on all these years? It felt as though she was waking up from a deep sleep and feeling her body come to life for the first time.

When he pulled his mouth from hers all too soon, she felt the loss keenly, as though going from the warmth of a fire to the bitter cold.

He uttered something harsh and guttural in a foreign language before she felt herself being unceremoniously hauled away from the dance floor towards the private area at the back of the club. Still dazed by the earth-shattering kiss, she didn't think to protest, allowing herself to be steered into a semi-private booth shielded partially from view by a thick red velvet curtain.

'I didn't mean for that to happen.' He spoke harshly, his breathing slightly laboured. 'I didn't intend to—'

'Please, don't apologise,' she blurted, not wanting his regretful words to taint what had been such a wonderful moment for her. One half of her prayed silently that he would leave, while the other half wanted nothing more than for him to take her in his arms again. 'I kissed you, after all.' She forced a smile. 'And I'm glad that I did.'

'You might not feel that way if you knew who I was.' He spoke evenly, but his expression held a trace of darkness that had not been there before.

'Maybe it adds to the sense of mystery.' She attempted a smile.

'Is this what you were seeking tonight, coming here?' His voice was a low rumble as he took a step closer. 'Kissing strangers on a darkened dance floor?'

Something in his eyes brought gooseflesh to her exposed skin. She couldn't put her finger on it but the atmosphere no longer felt warm and anonymous; she felt suddenly exposed and thoroughly out of her depth. The realisation of what she had just done came crashing upon her like a cold shower and she took a few slow backwards steps.

'Thank you for the dance,' she murmured, avoiding his eyes. 'It was…wonderful.'

He raised one brow, leaning against the side panel on the wall. 'Time to return to reality already?'

Cressida nodded once, feeling a strange pull between needing to get away and desperately wanting to stay. She wondered what his name was, where he came from. So many questions would be left unanswered once she left.

And still she walked away.

She left the club and its swaying music behind as she emerged into the night, the sharp wind making her wish she had brought a jacket. As she looked around to find where her chauffeur had got to, a trio of men in dark suits seemed to appear from nowhere.

'Your Highness,' the tallest one said in accented English, 'do not be frightened. We are ordered here to assure your safety.'

'My safety?' she breathed, looking around the street wildly. 'Where is my driver? How do you know who I am? Ordered by whom?'

'Ordered by me,' a familiarly accented voice rang out in the silent night from the nightclub doorway.

Cressida whirled, inhaling hard as she was met by the sight of the dark stranger from the dance floor walking towards her. Wordlessly, he draped a heavy woollen coat across her shoulders, guiding her a few steps away from the small army of what she presumed to be bodyguards.

His accented voice rang in her ears, intensifying the sensation of unease along her spine that warned her she had made a grave mistake tonight. She had overlooked something important. Her heart beat frantically in her chest as she met his dark gaze. 'Who *are* you?'

'I am Sheikh Khalil Al Rhas, ruler of Zayyar.' He held her pinned with his dark gaze. 'And you, Princess, are in a world of trouble.'

CHAPTER TWO

CRESSIDA FELT THE weight of his words settle somewhere in her chest. His accent, the way he had looked at her when they'd first spoken—it all fell horribly into place. 'You can't be him,' she breathed.

'And yet I am,' he said smoothly.

Disbelief held her body frozen for what felt like an eternity. Gone was the warmth from his eyes, replaced by a hardness that sent prickles along her skin.

She had sourced a few photographs online of the notoriously private Sheikh Khalil but the images she had seen had shown pictures of a man who seemed older, dressed in traditional white robes, his features obscured by a headdress and sunglasses. Not smooth shaven in a sleek open-collared suit, practically vibrating the air around him with a dark virility that made her knees weak.

This was her *fiancé*? The man her father had described as old-world and ruthless? She thought of all the anxiety that had plagued her, worrying what to say when they first met or how she should behave...

'Was this a game to you?' Her voice was suddenly ice-cold. 'Was it some kind of test to see how I might... perform?'

'No,' he said simply, a strange look crossing his features. 'This was most definitely not a part of my plan for our first meeting.'

Cressida swallowed hard. 'Did you know who I was from the start?'

His jaw seemed to tighten before he answered. 'Yes.'

'Well, then, I fail to see how you weren't toying with me.' She shook her head, unable to stand still a moment longer. She had taken no more than two steps towards the street and he was by her side. A muscular hand encircled her wrist, stopping her progress.

'Let me go,' she gritted, snatching her hand from him with force.

'You will not walk away from me, Princess,' he said softly. 'We have not yet finished our conversation.'

'I most certainly am finished. I never want to see you again.'

His mouth hardened into a thin line. 'You can come with me calmly so that we can resolve this privately, or you can make things needlessly difficult.'

As she watched, his eyes drifted to the handful of men surrounding them. She felt the distinct sensation of being caged in and it was not pleasant. 'Where is Frank?' she asked quietly, suddenly worried for her loyal chauffeur.

He raised one dark brow. 'Your driver has been relieved of his duties, along with your incompetent bodyguards.'

'You can't do that,' she breathed, aghast. 'They are not at fault for my actions.'

His head cocked to one side. 'It's a little late for remorse now, don't you think? If a driver can be persuaded to overlook protocol by a pair of fluttering lashes, then he has no business being entrusted with the responsibility.'

'You can't do this.'

'Oh, I most certainly can,' he purred, encircling her wrist with his strong hand.

'For tonight, at least, your safety is my responsibility.'

She did not know why, shock perhaps, but she put up virtually no fight as he guided her into the limousine that lay in wait by the roadside. The team of guards retreated into their own imposing vehicles to the front and behind. Even when it became clear that they were driving in completely the opposite direction to her apartment, she could not speak. She felt cold, the skin on her arms prickling with gooseflesh.

If her driver and guards had truly been dismissed, then that meant they would have already alerted King Fabian. Her father had already made it clear that he was depending on her to ensure this union went ahead at any cost. Guilt gnawed at her stomach as she closed her eyes, focusing on the gentle sway of the car to distract herself from the many reasons why, once again, she was an utter disappointment to her parents. This was the first and only thing the King had ever asked of her directly, the first time he had spoken to her since...well, since he had decided she was no longer worth speaking to. She had finally been given an opportunity to prove herself, to save her kingdom. And, as per usual, she had failed spectacularly.

'Are we to travel in silence?' The Sheikh was facing her, one long leg propped over the other, making him seem larger and more imposing in the small space.

'I fail to see how making idle chit-chat with you

will make this situation any easier.' She purposefully directed her gaze out at the passing blur of streetlamps and shadows.

'You seem quite indignant for someone who chose to run away from her guards for a wild night out.' His voice held only the smallest hint of impatience.

'I am not the one who did anything wrong here.'

'Aren't you?' He met her gaze evenly.

Before she could retaliate, the car came to a stop outside one of the most exclusive hotels in London. They were escorted inside by the Sheikh's entourage, who shielded them both from view until they were safely inside a private lift.

The Sheikh's suite spanned the entire top floor of the building, offering a breathtaking view of the London skyline. She was instantly drawn to look out at the majestic sea of lights of the city she had spent virtually no time exploring in the past five years.

She was aware of the bodyguards moving around as they performed a thorough check of the rooms. A handful of other men and women appeared briefly, speaking to the Sheikh in a language she assumed to be Zayyari. Her studies had included most European languages, along with ancient Greek and Latin, but she had no experience of Middle Eastern tongues. The way the syllables cut and rolled off their tongues was fascinating; it was a struggle not to turn and observe the conversations.

After a while she became aware of the lack of noise in the open-plan living space. She turned just as he reached her side.

Sheikh Khalil cleared his throat gently. 'Have you

spent all of this time appreciating the view or plotting on ways to escape, I wonder.'

She turned to face him fully. 'At what point did I become your prisoner?'

'Despite how others may portray me, I am not a tyrant. I assured your family that I would escort you to Monteverre personally and I will not go back on my word, even if you choose to end our arrangement.'

His gaze travelled briefly to her mouth before returning upwards. Did she imagine the slight dart of his tongue to moisten his lips before he spoke again?

He took another step so that he was by her side, one hand braced on the glass. 'I came to London to meet my future Queen on neutral ground. To ensure that we might begin our union on equal footing and avoid history repeating itself. It seems I'm destined to fail on that point.'

Cressida lowered her gaze, knowing he was referring to his failed engagement with her older sister, Olivia. The fact that she was a replacement bride should offend her, but she couldn't blame him for wanting Olivia as his first choice. Her sister was graceful and beautiful with a flawless talent for public speaking. Who wouldn't want her as their Queen? The arrangement between Monteverre and Zayyar had been in negotiations for months until her sister had chosen to walk away before accepting the proposal.

'You are our last chance, Cressida. Make me proud.'

'Tell me why you didn't reveal yourself straight away,' she said, ignoring the echo of her father's voice in her mind and firmly throwing down the gauntlet between them. She simply could not go ahead with the deal if tonight had been some kind of practical joke.

She had *some* pride. But could she truly return to Monteverre a failure?

'It was interesting to find myself meeting you without the complication of my own identity in the way,' he said simply.

'You see yourself as a complication?' she asked quietly, mulling over his words.

'When seeing a person as they truly are, yes.'

She raised her brows at his honesty. She knew all too well how the world changed once people knew you had a title in front of your name. Sometimes for the better, sometimes for the worse.

'I am not in the habit of using women as toys to amuse myself—was that what you accused me of?' He raised one brow in challenge. 'However, I will admit when I am wrong. I should have immediately announced my identity once I realised you had no idea who I was.'

'Yes. You should have.' She bit her bottom lip, trying not to look at him directly lest she be overtaken by another flashback to what it had felt like to be in his arms.

'But perhaps none of that matters, as you have said you are finished with all of this and never wish to see me again.' There was no playfulness in his words as he moved across the room to take a seat in the living area. 'Truthfully, this entire deal has been a fiasco from the start, with your father's lies and manipulations. It's clear to me now that you can't have been entering into this marriage willingly if this is how you choose to spend your free time.'

Cressida felt a prickle of irritation rise within her at his easy reclined posture and flippant judgement. There was no way she was going to beg this arrogant man to honour their agreement. And yet she was not quite ready to return to Monteverre if that meant her father lost the deal that would salvage their kingdom's failing economy.

She settled for a nonchalant shrug of her shoulders. 'This is an unusual situation for me, Your Highness, not that it's any of your business.'

'Perhaps both of us acted on impulse, Princess. But still, now I've met you I can't see how you will be happy away from the freedom and thrills of this kind of life. I have a duty to my people to give them a Queen who will be fulfilled by her role.'

'Why not just leave me here, then?'

'I am taking you back to your kingdom, just as I promised I would.' He watched her, his expression entirely unreadable. 'Your father made it very clear that your time in London had come to an end. But, considering recent events, I also made sure to consult my own sources. They told me that you are no longer enrolled with the university and the lease on your apartment has been cancelled.'

Her father had been quite busy this past week. He had not been happy when she'd told him of her wish to accept the teaching position, even before Olivia had walked away from the deal with the Sheikh. Cressida swallowed hard, moving to take a seat directly across from him in the luxurious living area. She had been fully prepared to return to her home country right up until approximately two hours ago. Why all of a sudden did it seem more favourable to walk through hot coals than to set one foot on Monteverrian soil?

She straightened her shoulders, making direct eye contact with the man across from her for the first time since they had entered his suite. 'I know that you have spent months on these negotiations. My father told me that you had already begun to invest millions, according to the deal, before my sister walked away from the arrangement.'

His eyes narrowed slightly, the rest of his expression utterly still. Clearly he'd had practice in holding his reactions in check.

Cressida crossed one leg idly over the other. 'It's clear to me that both our kingdoms stand to lose if we walk away.'

He was thoughtful for a long moment. 'There is much at stake. But tonight has made me question some things. I did not expect you to be a saint, Princess. You have clearly lived a life of…freedom…during your time here.' He looked at her pointedly. 'But a man in my position requires one hundred per cent loyalty from the woman by his side. To project an image of stability and unity.'

She chewed on the inside of her lip, fighting the urge to shout that she had never even kissed a man before tonight, but she resisted. 'I would like to propose that tonight should not have any bearing on our arrangement.'

'And yet it does.' He cleared his voice, angling his face away from her. 'There was something between us tonight—an attraction. A political agreement such as this one does not mix well with emotional involvement.'

'You think I am emotionally involved after one kiss?' she asked.

He tensed. 'I mean that sometimes people tend to read more into simple physical chemistry.'

And by *people* he meant *women*, clearly. She fought against the urge to roll her eyes. 'I am not one of those *people*,' she said pointedly. 'I don't particularly do emotional connections. I have always been perfectly happy with my own company.' She didn't tell him that it wasn't really her choice to be so cold, simply a part of her make-up.

The Sheikh stood, pacing to the sideboard at the corner of the room and pouring himself a glass of iced water. 'So if I am willing to go ahead with the arrangement, you wish to uphold your end of the bargain?'

Cressida took a deep breath, mulling over her words carefully before she spoke. 'I think I would be willing, but only once I know that the terms will remain the same. That it will not be a…a true marriage.'

Khal paused at the slight tremor in the young Princess's voice. She sat perfectly poised on the low-slung sofa, long slim legs tucked demurely to one side. One would never guess she had been virtually plastered to his front less than an hour before. He cleared his throat, pushing the images from his mind. 'The legal agreements you have already signed state the general terms of the union. What they do not overtly mention is that absolute fidelity is required, along with every effort to maintain the perfect image. So while we might not be sharing a bed as man and wife, I assure you that I would still expect a true marriage.'

A strange look crossed her features. She took a moment of pensive silence before looking up to meet his gaze head-on. 'Are those rules the same for you?'

Khal let a moment of silence hang in the air. 'In my country, the act of marriage is not one that is entered into lightly, even one of a political nature. So yes, the terms of the union would apply equally to both parties.'

She stood, pacing towards the window and wrapping

her arms around herself before turning back to him. 'Well, then, I suppose I don't have any other questions.'

'You sound very eager to become my Queen, I must say.'

'It has always been part of my duty to my kingdom to marry advantageously, if required.' She shrugged.

'And abandoning your studies? That does not bother you?'

She frowned, looking away for a moment. 'It's almost as though you are trying to talk me out of this.'

'I'm making sure you won't bolt at the last minute,' he said plainly, seeing no need to mince his words considering the turn the night had taken.

Understanding dawned in the depths of her blue eyes. 'You are concerned that I will act as my sister did.'

'I am protecting my own interests, yes.'

She nodded, biting her lower lip. 'I don't think that my sister intended to behave as she did. The Olivia that I know was always true to her word.' She shook her head once, a frown marring her brow. 'I understand that you have a vision for your future wife. That Olivia fitted a certain mould. I must warn you that I have not been a part of public life for many years—'

'My team are aware of this and are prepared to help you in your new role.' He watched as she moved back to sit delicately on the sofa once more. It seemed as if she were unable to be still. 'You seem quite eager to perform your royal duties; it surprises me in someone who has not set foot in their kingdom for such a long time.'

Her shoulders stiffened slightly at his words. 'Of course I have personal reasons for agreeing to this marriage, Your Highness. They are my own, not ones forced upon me or held over me. All I can do is assure you wholeheartedly that I'm here because I choose to be.'

'That's more than enough for me,' he said smoothly as he stood and took the few steps to close the space between them so that he stood over her. She inhaled sharply, freezing as he reached into the pocket of the coat he had draped across her shoulders earlier. He withdrew a small black box and sat on the seat alongside her.

'I understand that this is the tradition in Monteverre?' He opened the ring box, revealing a delicate vintage ruby ring set in the finest gold.

'Oh…' Her eyes widened. 'There is really no need for…'

He took her hand, cutting off whatever she'd been about to say as he slipped the ring onto the correct finger and surveyed his handiwork. 'A perfect fit.'

She cleared her throat, frowning slightly as she blinked down at the sparkling gem nestled against her pale skin. 'Thank you.'

Khal was suddenly very aware of the intimacy of their position. He stood, clasping both hands together. 'We will stop first in Monteverre for a brief press conference, followed by an engagement party. The wedding will take place as quickly as possible, but likely will be in a few months' time to allow for planning and invitations.'

Cressida frowned. 'Oh… I hadn't realised the wedding would be a big event.'

'There is usually some fanfare when a King takes a woman to be his Queen.' Khal fought the urge to laugh.

'I was under the impression from your secretary that we would be married quickly, that's all. That time was important to you.'

'You have an objection to the timing of the marriage?'

'No, not at all. The sooner the better, really.' She shrugged. 'I just thought there would be some kind of spin put on it. A secret elopement or something.'

'You do not want a big public wedding?'

'Well, it's just… No offence, but you are hardly the most public of figures and I clearly have not lived in the spotlight. It might seem odd if we suddenly announce a big wedding. I don't even know who I would invite, other than my family.'

Khal frowned, considering the logic in her words. The plan had originally been formed to account for his first bride—it was true that Princess Olivia was much more of a public figure in the media than her reclusive sister. Once again, it seemed his plans were being thrown to the winds. But perhaps, this time, a change in direction might benefit him and help him to make up for lost time.

Cressida noticed that the Sheikh seemed suddenly distracted as he called for one of his assistants to show her to her room. She barely had a moment to bid him goodnight before she was swept away and shown into a luxurious bedroom. A fresh silky towelling robe and slippers lay draped on the bed and she wasted no time in stripping out of her tight dress and heels before flopping onto the giant bed in the most un-princess-like manner possible.

The events of the night seemed surreal in her exhausted state. Almost as if she was living in some alternate reality of her own life. She raised her hand into the air above her head, staring at the ruby glinting on her finger. He had slid the ring on her finger with such businesslike finality, and yet the touch of his skin on hers had set her pulse racing.

She closed her eyes against the onslaught of memories from the hours before. The feel of his hands on her waist as they'd moved to the music, that first electric touch of his lips against hers. She would never let him know that he had been her first kiss; that would make it matter somehow.

Which it didn't. It had just been a kiss. She closed her eyes, repeating the words silently to herself and letting the tiredness take over.

She was awoken before dawn and told that they would be travelling to the airfield immediately. The sky was still jet-black and the air frosty as she ascended the steps to a luxury jet bearing the Royal insignia of Zayyar. The Sheikh was already on board and conversing with a team of men and women in traditional Zayyari attire. He had changed into white robes and the elaborate headdress she had seen in pictures.

She was thankful that he'd had the foresight to have a small case of her belongings collected and delivered to her room during the night so that she didn't have to wear the red dress again. She had not expected him to think of her comforts. Or, more realistically, it was his assistant who had thought of her. She took a seat near the front of the plane, swiping through the news on her phone as she waited for the meeting to end.

'Cressida,' a familiar deep voice called to her from within the cocoon of staff.

She stood, making her way down the wide aisle to the long conference table in the middle of the aircraft.

The men and women of his staff bowed their heads, moving away and revealing their King, seated at the top of the table surrounded by official documents and paraphernalia.

'I had not realised you planned to fly to Monteverre at first light,' she said breathlessly, fidgeting with the hem of her simple white blouse. She felt ridiculously underdressed in her blue jeans and worn sneakers. Her more expensive royal attire was sadly out of date, considering she had not attended anything as Princess Cressida in years.

'Change of plan.' He looked up for the first time, pausing to sweep his gaze over her briefly. 'We fly directly to Zayyar.'

'You are not taking me home first?'

'I thought it best to take you home after we are married. Which will now be in two days' time.'

CHAPTER THREE

'Two days? As in forty-eight hours from now?'

Khal had kept his tone deliberately neutral, taking in her pleasantly flushed cheeks and tied back hair. She looked younger without all the make-up from the night before, her ash-blonde hair was now swept neatly back from her face in a tight elastic band. The austere style only served to draw more attention to her wide-set blue eyes and porcelain skin. Of course, the red dress of last night had been more expertly cut to show off her curves than the plain blouse and casual jeans she now wore but he could still see the delicate dip and flare of her waist. If he thought hard enough, he could remember how good those curves had felt under his hands only hours before...

Redirecting his wayward thoughts, he cleared his throat and focused on the papers in front of him. 'That is correct,' he said coolly. 'I ran your suggestion past my team last night, after you went to bed, and they took it quite to heart. It seems you may have averted us from a mistaken course of action indeed.'

'My suggestion?' she breathed, her eyes growing wider still.

'The change in PR operation, of course. You alone

spotted the likely backlash in public opinion. You were absolutely right to question it.' He nodded in her direction as though congratulating her on acing a project rather than bumping forward an entire wedding. 'You did say that you would prefer to get married as soon as possible.'

'Yes… I did say that.' She moved to a nearby seat and sat down heavily. She looked ashen all of a sudden, small and fragile in the large leather chair that cocooned her.

'You have an entire bedroom to yourself for the duration of the flight,' he said, motioning to a set of doors at the end of the main cabin. 'You can't have got very much sleep last night.'

She pursed her lips slightly. 'Thank you. I could do with some more rest.'

Khal felt a momentary flash of conscience as she disappeared through the doors but pushed it away. He had done what was necessary in bringing forward the date. He had made the best decision to protect his deal. The sudden sense of urgency he'd felt—to take her far away from the life she had led in London and back to his kingdom—was purely down to expediting matters and avoiding any more risk of her going back on the agreement. The sooner Princess Cressida was his wife, the sooner he could get back to the business of growing his kingdom's influence and doing what he did best.

Khal took the time alone to gather his thoughts, trying to shift the uncomfortable sensation that had settled in his gut. He felt completely unhinged, as though everything he had believed of himself was being challenged. This entire marriage debacle had done nothing but challenge him from the moment his advisors had suggested it as a solution to their problem with European trade.

From the start he had not been able to deny that an alliance with Monteverre made sense. The global perception of his country was vastly outdated, harking back to their war-torn history. Zayyar had enjoyed an age of peace and prosperity for almost a quarter of a century and still they hit wall after wall when it came to foreign politics. Monteverre was one of the oldest nations in the Western world; it had influence and sway and, best of all, it desperately needed help in the form of cash investments, due to years of spending far beyond its means. It was simple mathematics.

What was not quite so simple was the old Zayyari law that demanded a marital alliance between two highborn members of aligning kingdoms. His advisors had already been fighting a backlash from the older generation, who disagreed with their country's changing landscape. He needed a bride if he wished to avoid public uproar. Thankfully, King Fabian had assured him that arranged marriage for the royal descendants was still a firm practice in his kingdom. Khal was not overly fond of the King, but he had not believed him capable of coercing his own daughter to the point that she would run away to avoid a proposal.

Cressida had assured him that she was not being coerced as her sister had been, yet still he wondered what personal reasons drove her to accept a political arrangement. Clearly she had a strong sense of loyalty to her kingdom and her family. It did not take much imagination to picture her by his side, swathed in silks and jewels, hosting lunches and balls in the Zayyari grand palace for hundreds of guests from all over the globe.

The trouble was, he had imagined a cold marriage. So far, his response to his fiancée had been far from cold. He'd had a true marriage once, built on the foundations of love and companionship. He had no desire to try to recreate that, for many reasons.

But the attraction between them was a complication he had not foreseen. Five minutes with her in his arms and he had practically pulled her to the nearest private area, needing more. She had felt so good in his arms. Too good.

The moment that he had realised she was completely oblivious to his identity he had felt something awaken inside him that he had long buried. Suddenly his quiet political marriage had seemed a lot less straightforward. He had planned to sit and keep watch until she decided to leave of her own accord. Then someone had tried to dance with her and that small primitive part of him he tried his best to suppress had roared to life, moving in to claim what was *his*.

So much for changing his image of ruthless desert King.

He had not expected to be physically interested in the woman he married; it was not necessary to the arrangement, after all. His head was not usually turned by long legs and a short dress. But the moment he'd had her body pressed against his, he had felt his libido emerge from its self-imposed hibernation with a vengeance. He'd been possessed by the mad urge to press his lips to the soft parts of her neck and continue down... It had shocked him, the need.

The wedding would take place in two days. This time he had made sure of it. An iron-clad contract of law bound Princess Cressida to their agreement. If she went back on her promise, his financial investments into Monteverre's failing economy became null and void. Perhaps it was severe, but he couldn't take a chance on her backing out of the marriage just like her sister had. Not when the future of two countries lay in the balance. He was not a patient man, quite the opposite. He liked things to be done precisely when he planned. Soon he could get back to more important matters in his own kingdom.

Cressida tried to stifle a gasp as the helicopter lowered swiftly to the ground, depositing them on a crop of barren flatlands on the very outskirts of the Zayyari desert. Despite her attack of anxiety at the news that she would become Queen so soon, she had surprisingly managed to sleep for almost five hours before waking with a ferocious hunger. The rest of the flight had been spent nibbling on snacks and perusing some of the books she had found on board about her new home, the desert kingdom of Zayyar. It had been a smooth trip from the private airstrip and she had presumed that they would arrive directly at the palace in the centre of Zayyar's capital city of the same name. Her Internet research had provided her with some basic facts of what to expect from her new home, but nothing could have prepared her for the heat. Her blouse already felt damp on her back as Khal helped her out of the SUV and into the direct glare of the burning hot sun.

She had covered her hair with a pale pink scarf before they exited the jet, provided by one of his many assistants. In general, Zayyar was rather cosmopolitan for the Middle East; they did not enforce modesty among the women of its population. But apparently where they were going for their wedding ceremony was a sacred place. It was all very mysterious.

'We continue on horseback from here.' Khal's voice was gruff and sleep-worn as he gestured to where his guards had already begun to mount impressively large dark steeds. 'You will ride with me.'

She gulped, taking in the sheer size of the animal before her. She had never been one for horseback riding as a girl. But, before she could object, strong arms gripped her hips tight and she felt herself being swung up onto the saddle as though she weighed nothing at all. The hard warmth of the Sheikh's chest pressed tight to her back as he settled behind her and she felt her body tense. The effort of keeping her eyes on the horizon was a welcome distraction as they began a swift gallop across the sand. There was no sound around them other than the beating of hooves on the dry desert plain. Gone was the hustle and bustle of city life she had grown used to, the noise she had used to distract her just as much as the books she lived inside. The air she breathed in was warm and fragrant, reaching deep within her and calming her raging heartbeat.

The thought that she had spent the past five years in one city was suddenly ludicrous. There had been a whole world outside her self-imposed cage, waiting to be explored. They crossed the endless expanse of sand for almost an hour; her thighs ached from stopping herself from relaxing back into the warmth of the hard male chest behind her. She still thought of him as the Sheikh, she realised. Surely one should be on first name terms with the man you were about to marry? He shifted his body behind her in the saddle, keeping the horse in pace. She felt gravity press her backwards until every inch of her back was plastered to his hard torso. All at once she felt the heat of him seep into her skin, sending goosebumps down her arms. It took all her strength not to dart away from the sensation, away from the overwhelming urge to sink further into it.

Clearing her throat, she turned her head to dart a quick look up at him. Her throat dried at the vision of his hard jaw in profile as he focused on guiding the powerful stallion up the dunes. Clearly he was not as affected by the ride as she.

All thoughts of him were momentarily curbed as their small party crested the last dune and a vision of beauty spread out in the valley below them. Golden sands gave way to the lush green paradise of a small oasis. Nestled in the middle of trees and ancient stone pillars were colourful Bedouin-style tents and temporary structures.

'Welcome to the sacred ground of Old Zayyar,' the Sheikh announced beside her ear. One strong arm snaked around her waist to hold her in place as they began their descent down the steep rocky hillside. They were greeted by a crowd of men and women in traditional robes and clothing, the men in elaborate headdresses and the women adorned in beautiful paints and jewels.

Men banged drums as the Sheikh dismounted and lifted her down to the ground in one powerful movement. She felt entirely out of place in her T-shirt and jeans combo.

'This is your bridal party,' the Sheikh said softly in her ear over the sound of the music and babbling. 'My young cousins speak a little English. You will be taken care of.'

A young woman stepped forward as if on cue, bowing low. Cressida shook her head and raised her hand, preparing to tell the woman not to make such a fuss.

'You are to be my Queen, Cressida.' He spoke once more. 'Be prepared to be treated as such.'

She nodded, straightening her shoulders as the rest of the women in the crowd bowed low in the same fashion. Her chest tightened with anxiety, feeling so many eyes on her, but she forced herself to take a step forward and then another, following the young woman into a large tent and leaving the rest of the crowd, and the Sheikh, behind.

Evidently it was customary for her to meet and join hands with every single woman in the tribe, each one offering what she hoped were kind words in their native tongue as they inked delicate patterns of henna on her skin. The women seemed warm and welcoming, despite the language barrier between them. She was acutely aware of her own plain Western clothing amongst their colourful draped fabrics. She caught more than one woman staring or whispering behind her hand when they thought she was not looking.

Her self-appointed assistant, Aisha, was a young woman of around twenty who had begun studying English only the year before. In between the courses of their evening meal, Aisha told her how she had sourced books and studied alone for a time before applying for a scholarship to university.

'The Sheikh's first wife was a great patron of female education. I thank her in my prayers each morning and night,' Aisha gushed before biting her lip suddenly. 'Oh, how thoughtless of me to mention such a delicate matter on the eve of your wedding!'

Far from being offended, Cressida's curiosity was piqued. She had already seen from her online research that the Sheikh had been married once before. That his wife had died in a tragic car accident four years previously. He had not mentioned her in any of their conversations so far and she did not see the point in bringing up what was likely to still be a delicate subject. 'I confess that I don't know very much about the late Sheikha. I have read that she was much beloved?'

'Sheikha Priya.' The young girl nodded, a wistful smile crossing her lips. 'She was…truly beautiful. She helped many people…' Tears filled the young woman's eyes and she wiped them away, apologising profusely.

'Please, don't apologise. Her death must have come as quite a shock to everyone.' Cressida felt her chest tighten as she offered a napkin to the young woman.

'It was a terrible time for Zayyar. Her Highness was so young. And of course His Highness was the victim of such scrutiny afterwards…because of the rumours.'

Cressida nodded, not wanting to admit that she had no idea what these rumours entailed. She felt the urge to press further, to find out exactly how many secrets lay buried under the facade of her simple marriage of convenience. She allowed the temptation to pass, exhaling as the conversation flowed amongst the women around her and the meal was served.

After dinner she was inundated with gifts of vibrant fruit baskets, decorated sweet cakes and fragrant teas, flowers and little bottles of oil as traditional music floated on the air. Aisha dutifully explained the symbolism behind each of the gifts, how they strengthened the couple's love for one another or brought fertility to the marriage. Cressida tried her best to ignore her discomfort at the thought of accepting such beautiful gifts, as neither love nor fertility would play a part in her marriage. She wished she could just tell them all not to make such a fuss, that she was not a real bride. That this was not the romantic fairy tale elopement that it seemed. She had always hated being in the spotlight and it seemed impossible to avoid as the women argued over her hairstyle and made final adjustments to her wedding clothes.

As night fell across the encampment, Cressida was finally left alone in her bridal tent. She could feel the strain in her cheeks from the polite smile that she had kept plastered on her face all afternoon. Her reflection in a nearby mirror showed dark shadows under her eyes, making her already pale skin seem even more translucent. She exhaled slowly, removing the pink scarf that covered her hair and combing it out with her fingers while ignoring the rising anxiety within her.

She had not been aware of any scandal in Zayyar's past when she'd committed to the marriage, but it made sense if that was the reason why Sheikh Khalil would go so far for a bride with Western ties. She had known from the bare facts available on the Internet that he was a widower, but, apart from a few vague news articles, that seemed as far as the information went. There was no further mention of the Sheikh's activities in the years since then. But she had noticed the way his staff hurried around him on the plane…as though he was a man to be feared.

So why did she not feel that same fear when she looked at him? She thought of the shivers that had run down her spine as he'd held her close on the horse ride across the desert, mere hours before. She had felt the opposite of fear; she had never been more excited in her life. She closed her eyes, placing one hand on her chest to feel the steady beat of her heart. No, she most definitely was not afraid to marry the Sheikh. She was more afraid of the intense attraction she felt every time he came close. Five years was a long time to spend trying to maintain her distance. He would find it easy, no doubt.

She straightened her shoulders, meeting her own gaze in the mirror once more. This was a job, she reminded herself. This was her duty. She would prove her loyalty to her family once and for all and make up for the mistakes she had made in her youth. Then she would be free to live her own life without guilt. She would be free of constantly feeling like a failure.

She moved to her bed, burying herself under the silk coverlet and closing her eyes tight. He had been her first kiss—it was only natural that she would be slightly affected by that milestone. She was not made of stone, much as she had tried to pretend she was. But she would not fail at this. If a cold, distant marriage of convenience was what the Sheikh of Zayyar wanted, then that was exactly what he would have.

The royal events team had worked quickly under pressure, creating a simple space that mixed elements of Western and Zayyari wedding cultures. Already the PR officials were drafting articles for the handful of magazines and newspapers who would be 'leaked' the news of the secret nuptials. The Princess had been right.

A large wedding would not have had half as much impact as this would.

Their marriage was to be a seamless union of east and west, a romantic desert fairy tale…or something like that. He had stopped listening to the event planner after she had begun talking about using sand as symbolism for their everlasting love. Little did they know how very far from the truth that was.

Khal stood in the heavy stillness of the desert air, watching as the sun began to dip low in the sky as evening fell upon them. The sand burned orange outside the intimate wedding tent and on the light breeze he could smell the fragrant pink flowers that had been arranged in vases and overflowing baskets all around the encampment in celebration. He picked one from a basket, simply to have something to do with his hands while he waited.

Priya had ordered similar flowers for their wedding day, he mused, the thought catching him off guard. He had ordered thousands of the blooms to celebrate their first anniversary. He crushed the delicate blossom in his hand, letting it fall to the ground as though it burned him. Of all the places for this farcical ceremony to take place, of course it would be here—they were in the very spot his parents had married. The sacred heart of his tribe and all the beliefs they held dear. A grand statement to the people of Zayyar, according to the team of advisors who had planned everything.

Priya had wanted a grand event, opting for a lavish three-day celebration in the Grand Palace. He steeled himself, willing his mind to change course. He could not think of his first wife, not when he was set to marry another at any moment.

Once they had arrived in the camp the day before, he had not wasted time in dispatching his fiancée to the women of the tribe, simply to put distance between them after the torture of the journey from the jet. In hindsight, opting to have her soft warm curves cradled between his thighs on horseback for an hour had not been his cleverest idea. He'd spent the afternoon riding across the desert to clear his head, cursing the lack of freezing cold lakes in their vicinity. He was not a teenager. He would not have his position made weak by his physical desire for the woman set to become his wife.

It was his own fault, for not taking a mistress in the years since Priya's death. He had always found an excuse not to move on—there had always been some battle to fight. Whether it was trying to find out the truth behind his wife's death or working against the economic repercussions of the rumours that had plagued him in the aftermath—that he had somehow been responsible for his wife's sudden demise.

He exhaled hard. He was a man. He had needs. And this was clearly the result when one suppressed those needs for too long. His fiancée was the very last person he could afford to desire right now. And the duty their marriage was based on made his situation even more difficult. He had demanded fidelity of her for the duration of their marriage; it was only fair that he offer the same loyalty himself. He would not risk the credibility of their union simply to slake his lust elsewhere.

His jaw felt as if it was made of stone as he heard a hush fall around the small gathering inside the tent. The event planners signalled that the bride was about to arrive. Khal stepped directly underneath two pillars swathed in snow-white gossamer fabric and watched as the small congregation of people appeared over the dunes. The single photographer who had been granted press access to the camp stepped forward, lens primed to catch the story of the year.

Khal kept his breathing steady, determined to play the part of calm groom. The people believed this to be a true marriage, after all. A romantic elopement between their King and his beautiful Western Princess. She was somewhere in the middle of the women, walking the same path that this tribe had walked for centuries. His jaw tightening painfully, he turned away and waited.

She reached his side with a whisper of silk flowing in the breeze, bringing the scent of jasmine and vanilla to his nostrils. Khal looked down and felt his breath catch for a moment. She was beautiful; there was no doubt. Pale porcelain skin offset by a shimmering golden wedding robe and heavy bejewelled veil. Was it a trick of the light or did her blue eyes seem to glow as she met his gaze?

Inhaling past the sudden tightness in his chest, he took his bride by the hand and began repeating his vows, his eyes never leaving hers. Part of the vows included a short sentence in Zayyari; he watched the concentration on her face as she vowed to be his for the remainder of their lives, a strange feeling within his chest as she did not stumble over the thick syllables of his native language. Their eyes met as the celebrant spoke of loyalty and devotion, of sharing a lifetime with one another. He looked in her eyes as the weight of their vows hung heavy in the air. And yet, as she promised to be true, he knew she spoke the truth. A strange feeling of calm came over him as he slid a wedding band onto her slim finger. A sense of complete victory.

Kisses not being customary at Zayyari weddings, they sealed their vows with a symbolic touching of foreheads. All too soon, he left the wedding tent with his new wife by his side to the rapturous applause of the small crowd. He watched as the new Sheikha bowed her head in delicate thanks as men and women complimented her beauty and good fortune in a language she did not understand.

Sayyid appeared by his side, clapping one hand on his back in solidarity. 'You seem happy, my King.'

'Do I?' he murmured, keeping watch as Cressida bent to take the hands of a group of children gathered around her. Security was tight and the people of the camp were peaceful, but still he resisted the urge to drag her away to privacy.

'You have barely taken your eyes away from your new bride. Am I to assume your concern is that she does not run away?' Sayyid smiled good-naturedly.

Khal smiled at the joke, brushing it off. He watched her because she was in a new country, entering a new life. He wanted her to feel at ease. And if he seemed happy it was because everything was going to plan, the lightness in his chest was a result of sealing a deal months in the making and securing the political future of his kingdom. Nothing more. He ignored his Chief of Security's raised eyebrow and returned to his wife's side as they continued to the celebration.

She had been told that celebrations in the camp usually lasted well into the night but not long after they had finished dining Khal leaned into her ear. 'Now it is time for us to make our exit and move to the ceremonial wedding tent.'

Her eyes snapped up to meet his. 'Just the two of us?'

'Don't look so excited, my Queen.' He made a motion with his hands to his guards that they were leaving before extending his hand to her. 'We must at least appear to be newlyweds who cannot wait to tear each other's clothes off.'

Cressida cleared her throat, staring at his outstretched hand and willing herself to stop being such an absolute coward. 'Can the King not make an exception to tradition?'

'Tradition is important to me,' he said simply. 'And it is even more important to the people of this sacred tribe. My family's tribe.'

'Of course.' She nodded, looking around at the small gathering of men and women, seeing how they looked towards their Sheikh's every move. And hers too, she realised with a sudden jolt. She had not thought much of the responsibility that came with her marriage. She was the Queen now, Sheikha of the realm.

Gulping, she stood as gracefully as she could muster. Khal bowed his head to the crowd once and she copied the motion, trying not to jump as the men suddenly shouted their approval in guttural tones. Raucous applause and what she presumed to be words of encouragement followed them across the sand as she followed Khal, flanked by four silent guards. The jewels on her veil tinkled gently as she moved forward, her skirts gathering around her legs with the effort of trying to keep up with the pace of the men and their much longer legs. Thank goodness she had not been forced to wear heels as well as the intricate dress.

From the outside, the tent had seemed just like the one she had stayed in the previous night. But as they stepped through the entryway Cressida went completely still.

If she had ever been the kind of person to hold romantic notions about her wedding night, this would probably be a fairy tale come to life. Swathes of jewel-toned fabrics cascaded from the intricately patterned roof, softly lit by traditional lamps and coloured lanterns. More lanterns provided a glow at strategic points around the space. Warm, luxurious Persian-style rugs carpeted the entire floor and the sensual scent of incense wafted through the air. But what drew her eye most was the enormous canopied bed of luxurious shimmering golden cushions that dominated the room. Filled with satin tasselled throw pillows and covered in bright red rose petals, it was as though it were created simply for the act of deflowering one's new bride. The thought made her gulp audibly.

'Leave us,' Khal commanded after two of his men performed a sweep of the tent's surprisingly large quarters. Once again, she felt slight unease at the level of security that preceded every move they made. She wondered at the reason for it; Zayyar had been at peace for almost a quarter of a century. But, before she could think too much of it, two things suddenly stopped her in her tracks. One, they were completely alone in the most romantic place in the entire world. And two, her new husband had removed his headdress and was shrugging out of his robe with surprising speed.

CHAPTER FOUR

NAKED FROM THE waist up, the man was like one of the statues she would stare at in the palace gardens when she lived in Monteverre. He had the body of a warrior, not a pampered king. He wore his hair long and unruly under the traditional head covering. Cressida whirled to put a few more feet of space between them, pretending to be suddenly interested in the array of fresh drinks and fruit laid out in the small dining area.

When she looked up once more, he had changed into a simple robe and loose drawstring pants, leaving only part of his chest bare. She gulped, looking away from the smooth mahogany skin and wondering when on earth she would regain control of her mind again.

'A robe has been laid out for you as well, and a private area for you to change.' He remained facing away from her, of which she was thankful. She moved quickly behind the screen, immensely grateful that her Zayyari bridal gown was nothing like the Western million-buttons-down-the-back variety. One simple zip ran down the side seam and she was free, stepping out of the pool of fabric and hanging it carefully.

It was a beautiful gown, so simple and elegant that she had almost felt beautiful for the first time in her life.

She had spent a lifetime being the ugly duckling, always comparing herself to her more attractive sisters. Eleanor and Olivia had vibrant red hair like their famous grandmother, the late Queen Miranda, who had once been named the most beautiful woman in the world. Cressida hadn't even inherited her mother's pale blonde locks, instead ending up with an in-between shade of ash-blonde that was entirely forgettable. But the shade of her wedding gown and the sparkling amber jewels that adorned it had made her glow from head to foot.

A standing mirror faced the screen; she angled her body sideways, hardly believing that the woman in the glass was her own reflection. Her lingerie was the same dusky golden shade as her dress but stitched with shimmering embroidery that drew the eye to the illusion of her much fuller breasts. Closing her eyes firmly at the thought, she pulled the buttery soft silk robe over her shoulders, crossing it at the waist and noting that it was significantly shorter than the male version. No drawstring trousers were provided for the bride, it seemed, leaving her legs completely bare from mid-thigh downwards.

Perhaps it was the sensually charged décor of the tent or simply the overwhelming romance of the day in general, but suddenly she felt flushed and hyper-aware of the silk material as it moved against her skin. She felt a strange tightening in her solar plexus at the thought of stepping beyond the screen and revealing her ensemble to the man who was now her husband. She wanted him to see her, she realised with sudden heat in her cheeks.

She wanted him to look at her like he had in London and she wanted to find out just what it felt like to have his hands on her again. But it was unlikely that whatever madness had existed in the dark in London would be present now. He had made it clear that they would not have a true marriage, had he not? With a shake of her head she pulled the robe as tight as it would go, successfully covering most of her cleavage but still leaving much of her legs on show. Opting to leave her hair down, she took a deep breath and stepped back into the open space of the tent, only to find Khal standing opposite her, the ridiculously sensual bed spread out between them like a battlefield.

If only she could have simply turned tail and ducked back behind the screen, just to avoid the treacherous pang of heat that ran down her spine. His eyes raked over her, moving slowly to take in her hair, her breasts, then finally resting upon her bare legs.

Unable to stand still under his scrutiny, Cressida willed herself to move past the bed, turning her back on him on the pretext of pouring herself a glass of water.

'If you plan to continue skittering around me it is going to be a long night.' He sat down and sprawled back on the bed, hands interlocked behind his head as he surveyed her.

She moved forward, stumbling over her words as she nervously twisted the tie of her robe between her fingers. 'I can sleep on the futon if you'd like to take the bed.'

'And have all of the servants know we spent our wedding night apart?' He sat up, both hands braced on his knees. 'We will share a bed for tonight.'

Cressida nodded once. 'Of course. I didn't think…'

'Am I so frightening?' He watched her, waiting.

She placed her glass of water on the table, still twisting one ribbon of her robe around her finger. 'I am not afraid of you. I suppose I'm a little overwhelmed by all of this.'

His brow furrowed. Without warning, he stood and walked to a low table in the middle of the tent where an elaborate tea service had been laid out. He poured the steaming dark liquid into traditional cups and handed her one. 'You seemed to enjoy the festivities this evening. I had worried the Old Zayyari style might be a little far from what you are used to.'

Cressida smiled. 'I adored every moment. I have not travelled much before so this is all so new, but in a good way.' She took a sip of the strong brew, feeling it warm her through. 'I'm impressed at how quickly your team arranged everything.'

'The clandestine photographs will probably be making their way into the wrong hands as we speak,' he mused, one corner of his mouth lifting.

Cressida noticed a tiny dimple appear in his cheek, but it was gone almost before it appeared. He never smiled fully, she realised. It was as though he did not allow himself to. She pushed the thought away, realising that he was still speaking of the ceremony, oblivious to how her thoughts had wandered.

'They simply made some modifications where needed. This tent in particular was redesigned to be larger but the sanctity still lies in the markings on the cloth itself.' He pointed upwards to the domed roof.

She looked up, squinting at a jumble of blurry shapes on the cloth. She could not make out a single thing at a distance without her glasses.

'Looking for these?' He extended the blurry outline of her glasses towards her. She took them quickly as though any prolonged contact might ignite the spark that she was quite happy to ignore.

Cressida adjusted the frames on her nose, craning her neck upwards. Sure enough, the pattern was made up of more than just an arbitrary design. Spread out above them were thousands of intricate symbols and markings painted in burgundy-coloured ink on the raw canvas material. An ancient language. Her mind soared to life, all other thoughts abandoned as she kneeled on the edge of the bed to get a closer look. 'Fascinating…' she breathed. 'What do they all mean, I wonder.'

'I have absolutely no idea,' he said, shrugging. 'The markings are very old; they can be traced back to the first Zayyari tribe that made their settlement in this exact spot. Spending the wedding night here is an ancient custom that goes back to the very dawn of my people.'

'Absolutely fascinating,' she said, mostly to herself.

'Yes, you've said that already.'

She brought her gaze back to him. 'I'm sorry but this kind of stuff is exciting for me. I'm trying my best not to get out my phone to research ancient symbols on the university library database.' She paused, realising with a pang of sadness that she no longer had access to the database as she was no longer a student. Still, she forced a smile. 'Don't worry, I won't.'

'I'm thankful. What would my guards think of me if they walked in here and you were on your phone on our wedding night?'

'Oh, I doubt the signal is strong enough in the middle of the desert, anyway.' She smiled, hardly believing that they were having light conversation after the hyper intensity of the past two days. He still did not

smile but his eyes seemed warmer at least, more inviting, like they had at the bar the first time they'd spoken.
It seemed like another life, rather than mere days ago.

'I can assure you the signal would be perfect,' he
said, offhand. 'Zayyar trades in technology; it is the
lifeblood of our economy right now.'

'I read an article that called you an economic genius.'

'The success of this kingdom is a result of the
strength and knowledge of the members of government, the money that is put into educating our people
and ensuring their quality of life. I believe that when
you spend time on nourishing the foundations, growth
is inevitable.'

'My father seems to have a very different idea on the
measure of economic success,' Cressida said, tracing a
circle on the embroidered bedspread. 'When his advisors warned him that economic crisis was forecast, his
answer was to buy a new fleet of tanks for the military.
A show of wealth, he called it. As though pretending
debt was not a problem would simply make it true.'

'There are many leaders who think this way. My
great-grandfather was one of them.'

She knew a brief history of the kingdom and the wars
that had been waged two generations before. She could
see it on his face, the tightness that settled around his
eyes at the mention of his ancestor. 'It must be hard,
having that history to work against.'

'Not as hard as it must have been for those who lived
through it.' He became quiet then, his features turning hard.

'You care a lot about your kingdom,' she said simply.

'The same must be said of you, to have agreed to a
marriage in order to save it.'

Cressida shrugged, studying the markings on the ceiling to avoid his knowing gaze. 'There are not many things that third in line to the throne is expected to do, except remain free of scandal and marry according to the King's wishes.'

'And now King Fabian finds himself with only one direct heir...' Khal mused.

Cressida looked up, surprised that she had not thought of that fact. Now that Olivia had given up her place in line to the throne the duty fell entirely upon Eleanor to ensure there was a new generation of Sandovals to carry on the name. And the throne. 'My father is not known for his excellent decision-making skills.'

'Your sister will make an excellent queen,' Khal said earnestly. 'I do not doubt that the future of Monteverre is in competent hands.'

'They just need to survive the remainder of my father's rule.' Cressida smiled ruefully, worrying at her bottom lip. 'But thank you.'

She felt something bloom in her chest at his kind words. She had always looked up to her oldest sister for guidance as a child but she had never envied her position one bit. She had never harboured a desire to become Queen, knowing her strengths lay happily in academic work and keeping a low profile. Just look where that had got her.

'I must point out that you said that it was your duty to remain free of scandal, and yet in London...'

'I was not seeking scandal,' she said, her shoulders straightening. 'I just acted on impulse for the first time in my adult life. It made sense at the time.'

'And now?'

She felt it humming between them again, that sizzle

of awareness that she wished she could ignore. But the events in London had made that entirely impossible. She could not tell herself that the attraction was one-sided any more than she could tell herself that the earth was square. It was simply a fact, heavy in the air between them. Ever present in the tension that seemed to coil tight in her abdomen whenever she was in his presence.

'Now it is irrelevant.' She shrugged. 'I am…your wife.'

Something darkened in his eyes at her words. 'Indeed.'

The large bed suddenly felt too small, her body restless under his heated gaze. She turned her head away, murmuring a hasty goodnight as she tried to relax into the pillows. She was vaguely aware of him moving to extinguish some of the lamps in the tent before returning to the bed but she didn't dare open her eyes. Feigning sleep soon became effortless as the activities of the day caught up with her and sleep claimed her.

It was too hot, Cressida mused, turning over onto her stomach and feeling a sheen of sweat on her skin. The air in her nostrils was white-hot and strangely heavy in her lungs, almost painful. Her eyes snapped open, seeing a strange glow illuminating the room like dancing lights through a fog. Not fog, she corrected herself, smoke.

She felt drunk, consciousness sliding away from her like desert sand through her fingers. Sleep pulled her back, the strange dream melting away.

A man's voice shouted nearby in a language she could not understand, jolting her once more. Then she was being lifted from the bed into strong arms and carried at frantic speed. The strange fog suddenly became recognisable smoke in her lungs, the dancing lights the visible flames of a red-hot fire that was burning up one entire side of the tent. Suddenly the stars were above them and fresh oxygen filled her lungs, making her eyes water. She looked up and found herself eye level with Khal's strong jaw, his powerful body carrying her in a zigzag path through the encampment to where a trio of black dune buggies lay in wait. He deposited her onto the back seat, taking her face in his hands.

'Are you okay?' he breathed, his voice hoarse from smoke and exertion. 'Speak to me.'

'I'm… I'm fine, I think.' She coughed, shivering as realisation of what had just happened began to seep into her consciousness. The look on his face said it all—this was no accident. 'Are we in danger?'

He did not answer her question. 'We will be travelling under darkness but I will protect you. You will not step from my side until we reach the palace, understood?' He turned but did not remove his hand from where it lay on her forearm, waiting for the guards to catch up before he began issuing quiet orders. The men simply nodded, obeying their leader and preparing to depart. Khal slid into the seat beside her, draping one arm over her as they set off, a guard at the wheel. His face was only visible for a few moments before the complete darkness of the desert engulfed them and she couldn't help but grip him tighter. *'I will protect you,'* he had said. And she believed him.

He stayed by her side as they moved from buggy to helicopter, holding the woollen blanket around her the entire time. Preserving her modesty. She tried a few more times to ask what had caused the fire and was met with stony silence from both Khal and his guards. She was not to worry about that, they said. The lack of information only served to heighten her unease. The people of the tribe were peaceful; surely the fire had been accidental? And yet the look she had seen in Khal's eyes as they moved away from the desert was not one of annoyance at someone's foolish mistake. It was a look of absolute rage.

Soon the inky blackness of the desert below gave way to a sea of lights, main roads winding towards a large city. Once they had touched down within the old palace walls she felt Khal visibly relax beside her. Knowing that he had been worried the entire time gave her a sharp pang of anxiety.

An elderly servant appeared and offered, in perfect English, to settle Her Highness in the Sheikha's apartments. The sudden noise that came from Khal's mouth startled her. He gave a few commands in his native tongue and the servant nodded once and disappeared with quiet efficiency.

'Where will I be staying?' Cressida asked, surprised that her voice did not shake after the panic of their ordeal.

'With me. Where you will be safe,' he said simply. His hand was gentle but firm as he gripped her elbow, motioning for her to walk. The first pink fingers of dawn were beginning to snake across the darkness above them. She had barely got a glimpse of the courtyard of her new home before she was being led at speed along winding anonymous stone passageways, deeper into the heart of the palace.

Khal never let go of her arm. She was immediately aware when they entered a more modern wing, more refined and luxurious in its décor. The guards performed a quick sweep of the rooms around them before Khal motioned to dismiss them. He spoke one phrase to his own personal bodyguard; the large man nodded once and closed the door behind him with a soft thud.

'They need to clear the rest of the wing,' he said wearily, running a hand along the stubble on his jaw. 'I would like the doctor to see you before you rest.'

'I'm fine, Khal, honestly.' She shook her head. 'All I need is to sleep.'

'You called me Khal,' he said with surprise.

'I suppose *Your Highness* just seems a little too formal now that we're married. And you did just carry me out of a burning tent.' She felt laughter bubble in her throat, along with the irrational urge to burst into tears at the realisation that this man had probably saved her life tonight.

'You need to be seen by a doctor,' he repeated. 'There was a lot of smoke.'

Cressida nodded, remembering the thickness of the smoke filling her lungs, the burning heat prickling at her skin. Then she remembered how quickly she'd felt safe once she was in his arms, enveloped in his strength. Tears filled her eyes and fell down her cheeks before she even realised what was happening. She turned her face away quickly, not wanting him to see her weakness. But hiding was useless; he was by her side almost before the first tear fell, gathering her in his arms and holding her tight. A few choked sobs escaped her throat; she stifled them with her hand, embarrassed at her complete loss of control. 'I never cry,' she half sobbed, half laughed at herself.

'It's the shock,' he murmured. 'Just breathe.'

She obeyed his command, focusing on the warmth of his arms and the steady beat of his heart somewhere near her ear as she inhaled and exhaled. When she finally felt strong enough to step away, he surprised her by holding her still.

Cressida's stomach flipped at the look in his eyes as strong muscular fingers cupped her jaw. He considered her eyes with such fierce intensity that for one crazy breathless moment she wondered if he might kiss her. No sooner had the thought crossed her mind than his lips were on hers, hot and demanding. His hand fisted in her hair as he angled her to deepen the kiss while the other snaked around her waist to gather her against him.

Perhaps it was the adrenaline still coursing through her veins, or the reminder of her own mortality, but his touch was like kindling to a fire. She wanted to fall into the oblivion of desire and forget all the reasons why it was a bad idea. All she cared about was that there should be less robe between them and more touching. Much more touching. He pressed his thigh between her legs, pinning her to the wall as he kissed her so hard she was light-headed. But no sooner had she begun to sink into him than he was gone. He took two steps away, bracing one hand against the door as he got his breathing under control.

'We have both been through a lot tonight,' he said quietly, not meeting her eyes. 'You should go and get some rest. There are three guest rooms to choose from in my wing; choose whichever you wish.'

Cressida did not trust herself to speak, nodding once as she readjusted the front of her robe to cover herself. Clearly that kiss had just been the result of shock; she knew not to read too much into it. He had been more than clear that they would not behave as man and wife. But it seemed that her body had not received that message. She raised a hand to her face, feeling the blush creep as far as her forehead. The enthusiasm with which she'd kissed him made her blush deepen even further.

Her heart pounded furiously, the remnants of such a sudden flare of passion ebbing slowly away. He, on the other hand, seemed to have regained his composure with complete ease. Anger crept into the corner of her vision. How dare he be so cool and collected while she felt completely turned inside out? It wasn't fair.

A firm knock on the door dissipated what was left of the intimate moment and Cressida spun on her heel to pull her robe tighter around her. She didn't dare to look to see if Khal showed any physical signs of unfulfilled lust, focusing her gaze downwards to take in the patterns on the tiles under her bare feet.

'The adjoining rooms have been cleared.' Sayyid's voice came from behind her, in English for her benefit. 'Come with me, Your Highness.'

Khal made no move to speak or meet her gaze as she passed him; she tried not to feel hurt or rejected at his distance. He probably had many things to attend to other than escorting his new bride to her room. He was King, after all.

Steeling herself, she followed Sayyid to her bedroom and tried to ignore the sense of loneliness that rose in her with each step.

CHAPTER FIVE

'WHAT ON EARTH was His Highness doing sleeping in a tent in the first place? It's utterly ludicrous!' exclaimed the Minister of Defence. 'That encampment was likely filled with thugs and ruffians.'

'It is tradition. Part of the family legacy,' someone at the back of the room added.

Khal made his arrival known by clearing his throat, the sound seeming to cut through the unusual din in his official chambers. The emergency dawn meeting had been assembled by Sayyid, his Chief of Security, who currently looked as though he might like to tear a chunk out of the rather elderly Defence Minister.

'Gentlemen, take your seats,' he commanded, in no mood to deal with the squabbling that ensued with this many egos in one room. He hadn't slept since the encampment; the stench of smoke still clung to his skin, even after showering.

'Your Highness, we are deeply troubled to hear of this unfortunate incident,' the Chief of Police offered respectfully. 'I have assembled a team to investigate the site; they are en route as we speak.'

'Do we really need the police involved?' the minister intervened. 'I mean, we aren't sure of the origin of the fire. For all we know, it could have been a tribesman tripping over a lamp.'

'The King has expressed his wish for a thorough investigation,' Sayyid said loudly.

All eyes moved to him. Khal nodded once to confirm and watched as the men's attitudes changed instantly to rapt attention, some even taking notes as Sayyid outlined the security measures taken and the times of guard check-ins throughout the night.

'Your Highness, are you worried that there is unrest amongst the old orders?' An elderly man, one of his father's long-time advisors stepped forward. 'You once expressed the belief that they were behind the death of the late Sheikha Priya.'

'His Highness made those statements while experiencing enormous grief,' another advisor said pointedly. 'The Sheikha's death was deemed accidental.'

Khal felt the casual mention of his wife's death like a punch to his gut. He stood before he had the sense to rein in his anger. 'The investigation into my wife's death is still ongoing,' he hissed.

The elderly man shrank back visibly, realising he had overstepped the mark.

The Minister for Foreign Affairs spoke softly, addressing each of the men around the oval table in an effort to calm matters. 'Have a care for the language used in this chamber, gentlemen. All it takes is one whiff of scandal to cause an international spectacle.'

Khal turned from the table, unable to stand one more minute of their so-called politics. 'This meeting is over. Any questions about the incident will be addressed to my personal security team.'

He didn't know where he was going, anger powering

him along the ancient passageways until he finally felt
the sun on his face. Tension filled his veins, the effort
of holding back memories threatening to undo him. He
changed direction, moving towards the stables with sudden intent. He demanded his prize stallion to be readied
and wasted no time in switching his traditional robes
for tight-fitting jodhpurs and well-worn boots. He did
not speak to the boy who handed him the reins, impatiently launching himself up into the saddle and taking
off in the direction of the sand.

With the wind on his face and the pounding of hooves
under him, he finally allowed his spine to relax as he
moved with his horse, their bodies in tune as he pushed
the great beast to the limit. Takaa was a demon, the fast-
est horse he had ever owned, and right now he had never
been so tempted to test his limits. Knowledge made him
slow down as he got close to the boundaries of the old
palace lands, veering off down the hill to where an almost dried up ravine formed a small oasis of sorts.

Takaa drank deeply and Khal splashed water onto his
sun-warmed face, feeling the midday heat begin to claw
at him through his thin shirt. His fists were almost white
with the effort of suppressing the rage that had begun
to unravel inside him in the chambers. They spoke her
name as though it were a trivia, not a bomb that had the
ability to tighten his gut with emotion. Grief was an obvious one; he most definitely had allowed grief to sink
its mighty claws into him more than once in those first
months following Priya's sudden death. She had been
his wife for five years, his rock during his father's death
and his ascent to becoming the leader he was today.

Everyone had offered him condolences and comfort
and in time he had moved past it to the point where he

could return to normal life. But the anger was another issue entirely. How did one resolve anger that was soul-deep when the woman who'd caused it was being lamented by their people so much they built shrines to her in the streets? Poetry was written about her beauty, her grace.

He had been left virtually alone with the knowledge of who his wife truly was. How she had betrayed him and everything their marriage stood for. How he had driven her to that betrayal with his own over-controlling measures. How did he resolve the guilt and the regret that ate away at his very soul—that things had not been different?

He growled, throwing the nearest rock at the water so hard that Takaa startled and began to pull back at the reins. He placed his palm flat on the horse's neck, crooning low in his throat until the animal stopped resisting and leaned down to drink once more.

The memory of seeing the smoke last night, of rushing to get Cressida to safety while he was sure his heart would burst through his chest. It had brought him right back to the moment he had been told of the accident. It was as though, for a few moments of madness, both incidents had been one and the same and he was trapped in a nightmare of sorts. And then, when the danger had passed and he was sure she was safe and alive, holding Cressida in his arms while she fell apart had been almost more than he could bear. She was not a woman who lost control of herself easily; that much was painfully evident. And yet she had shown him her weakness. And how had he responded? By ravishing her at the first opportunity, beast that he was.

He had never felt such a challenge to his self-control

than when he was around her. With each encounter, it felt as though he were losing his grip on a cliff face one finger at a time. She was getting under his skin and it simply could not continue. The physical attraction between them was more than inconvenient. It was a risk to the business arrangement of their marriage. They needed to keep their roles clear so that the next five years passed without incident. She would be the perfect Queen as he required her to be and he would break down the various political walls that stood in the way of his development plans with ease. Then, once their time was up, they would part without difficulty or complication.

He mounted Takaa swiftly and kicked off back to the palace, a plan in place. He would resolve this situation just as he did every other area of his life, with careful management and the complete absence of emotion.

While the dramatic details of the reasons behind their late-night arrival were kept carefully under wraps, news of the new Sheikha spread through the palace quickly. Cressida was awoken at dawn by a handful of servants and a young dress maid, who set about draping her in traditional silks and jewels. Zayyari was not one of the languages taught in her university and she found it incredibly frustrating not being able to make out a single word of what the women said as they spoke to one another in low tones, avoiding her gaze. She had the strange feeling of being a new statue on display at a museum.

She made a mental note to begin studying as soon as possible. The thought of having something even remotely connected to her previous academic accomplishments made her feel slightly less at sea in her new life. She had always felt most comfortable when she planned her goals for each term and ticked items off one by one. As she was dressed and styled with hair and make-up, she mentally listed out the materials she would need to get started.

Just as she had begun on the prospect of brand-new stationery, an older woman entered and announced herself in English as her new assistant.

'You are expected to breakfast with the esteemed Sheikha Amala and Princess Nia this morning,' the older woman said, scrolling down the screen of a sleek tablet as she spoke. 'Your new mother and sister-in-law, as they are called in the West.'

'Where will that be?' Cressida asked, trying to conceal the sudden rumble of her stomach along with the fact that she had no knowledge of anyone in her husband's family.

'They live in the palace grounds,' Rana said simply. 'Then this afternoon we will commence your etiquette lessons, followed by cultural and language tuition.'

'Etiquette lessons?' Cressida repeated, her mind stumbling over the sudden weight of having an itinerary handed to her.

'His Highness has arranged for an intensive month of tuition to make you more comfortable in the run-up to your celebration ball.'

She was to be given a ball? As in, an entire event to celebrate her? She fought the urge to flap her arms at the woman currently applying make-up to her eyelids. This was too much to absorb while sitting completely still. Taking one deep breath, followed by another, she waited for the make-up artist to move away for a moment before narrowing her gaze on her new assistant. 'You said the Sheikh has arranged all of this?'

'Along with his team, of course. The priority right now is for you to feel as prepared as possible in your role as Queen.'

Or did the Sheikh himself simply wish for her to be kept as busy and out of sight as possible? Cressida wondered. She didn't know why she felt a sense of rejection that he had not chosen to at least eat breakfast with her in order to inform her of his plans. They had not spoken at all of what the day-to-day workings of their arrangement would be. He was not breaking any promises.

So why did she feel so utterly alone of a sudden?

She simply wished to ask for further news on the fire at the encampment, she told herself. She did not like being left in the dark on the matter. She would seek him out, perhaps. She would ask him for an update and perhaps clarify what was to be expected of her from this point, other than the ridiculous ball and the lessons he and a team of servants and tutors had apparently deemed necessary.

Finally, the make-up artist finished her work and stepped away. Cressida barely even glanced at her own reflection; she needed to stand and move and have a few feet of space to herself for the first time in two hours. The fact that it had taken two hours to get dressed was utterly ridiculous; she had always just put on an outfit, brushed her hair and gone about her day with minimal fuss.

'Is everything okay, Your Highness?'

Cressida looked up from the stifling weight of her thoughts to find all three women looking at her worriedly. She straightened, remembering herself, and plastered on the most serene royal smile she could muster in the face of her inner turmoil. 'I'm fine. Let's get started on the day, shall we?'

* * *

Khal's mother and sister turned out to be surprisingly warm and inviting. Their family apartments were smaller and slightly less formal than the Sheikh's wing. They made their introductions and she was hugged warmly by her new mother-in-law before they sat together to enjoy a warm breakfast of spiced breads, fresh fruit and hot Zayyari tea.

The Sheikha Amala was younger than Cressida had expected, a beautiful woman with perfectly applied make-up and eyes that shimmered with kindness. Princess Nia was only slightly older than Khal, with a family of her own. She spoke fondly of her two young sons, who attended an elite boarding school in Scotland for much of the year but returned to the palace for holidays. Khal's mother did not speak any language other than her own but the Princess conversed easily in both French and English and talked wistfully of her time abroad in Paris when she was younger.

After a time, the Sheikha's mood seemed to change as she began to speak with her daughter as translator, asking for details of the secret wedding ceremony. Cressida described the welcoming environment of the encampment, leaving out the details of the heavy security presence and the fire that brought the night to an abrupt close. No sooner had Cressida begun to describe her fascination with the symbolism on the wedding tent than the older woman stood with a loud sniff and excused herself from the room.

'Did I say something wrong?' Cressida asked the Princess, her worried gaze following her as the door snapped shut, leaving just the two of them.

'My mother is deeply unhappy that Khal did not

allow us to attend the wedding,' Nia said, taking a sip of her tea. 'He explained that it was necessary—it was to be an elopement, and none of the royal family would be present.'

'I am sorry.' Cressida bowed her head. 'It all happened very fast. I'm sure he would have preferred to have you there.'

Nia smiled sadly. 'I think she is upset because she knows that is not the case.' She pursed her lips. 'I have two sons. I know my heart would break to find one of them had shut himself off from me. My brother has been like a stranger to us these past few years. He grieved for a long time. I know it well, such grief. I lost my own husband after only three years of marriage. A loss like that leaves a hole in your soul.' Nia sighed. 'Grief can be so destructive…it takes a part of you with the one you lost.'

The young woman's eyes filled with tears and Cressida felt the urge to reach out and embrace her. Thinking that might be a tad too familiar for a first meeting, she settled for a single solemn pat on her hand. Nia smiled, wiping away the single tear that had escaped her heavily made-up eyes.

'I imagine it is not enjoyable to think of your husband when he was so entwined with another.' She winced. 'I did not think before I spoke.'

'Love is not a fundamental part of this particular marriage,' Cressida said carelessly, regretting the words as soon as they escaped her mouth. 'What I mean is…'

'It has not been disclosed by my brother, but I had a feeling that this had something to do with politics.' The Princess smiled. 'Don't worry; your secret is safe with me.'

'Thank you. And I'm sorry for your loss.'

The older woman shook her head gently. 'I am grateful for my position. I have my brother to watch over my sons as they grow into young men. I have time to spend with my mother, though she can be a little dramatic.' She laughed good-naturedly.

Cressida found herself smiling, a real smile. She liked Khal's sister very much and it was nice to know there was someone here to talk to who was not employed by Khal to watch over her or transform her into the perfect Queen. All too soon, their time was up and Nia rushed off to attend to her mother.

Cressida left the family apartments and trailed behind her assistant for an extensive tour of the palace grounds. The historical Grand Palace compound was almost three hundred years old but showed clear signs of renovation in certain places. Her assistant pointed out the renovations as scars of the wartimes when the palace had been damaged by rebels. Cressida thought of Khal and his determination to have his kingdom accepted by the world despite the violence in Zayyar's past. How many other areas of this beautiful kingdom had been destroyed and rebuilt?

In the cavernous portrait gallery, she was shown depictions of Zayyar's past rulers. Fierce-looking men with long beards and swords sheathed by their sides. As the paintings became more modern, she instantly recognised the face of Khal's mother, by the side of an older man. The old Sheikh had kind eyes, not too different from those of his son. The family resemblance was quite strong.

The next picture portrayed a young Khal alongside a beautiful raven-haired woman. Cressida paused, looking up at the picture of her husband and his original

Queen. She was a stunning beauty, all dark features and effortless grace. He was entitled to still be in love with his dead wife, she reminded herself. Theirs was not a marriage built on the pretence of love or even affection. If anything, it should make things easier knowing that he was emotionally unavailable.

She forced herself to move away from the shadow of the woman who had captured her husband's heart, knowing that such a matter should not concern her. She was an instrument of political influence, not a true wife, and she would be a lot happier if she kept that thought front and foremost in her head.

Learning a new language was her favourite pastime in the whole world, so when she sat down to her first Zayyari lesson with her personal tutor, naturally she expected to feel the same passion and excitement that always came over her with a new academic challenge. But after half an hour she still could not pull her thoughts away from her talk with Nia and the mysterious scandal of the late Sheikha's death. Seeing the picture of Khal with Priya had got under her skin. Why did she feel the urge to compare herself to the dark-eyed beauty? To wonder if Khal compared her too. She had already known that she was second choice to her sister Olivia to be his bride. She had been able to rationalise that as Olivia was older and more famous than she was.

But she could not rationalise how she felt in this moment. A sensation prickled in her chest, peculiarly like jealousy, and she pushed it away, throwing herself into her lessons for the day and determined not to think of the Sheikh at all.

Or his beautiful lost love.

CHAPTER SIX

THE NEXT DAY, once again, the Sheikh was nowhere to be found. Still, he made his presence known by ensuring she had meetings with various advisors whose sole purpose was to groom her to become his perfect Sheikha. She took another more detailed tour of the palace and grounds, accompanied by guards, of course, and tried not to be completely overwhelmed at the prospect of memorising the various winding mile-long corridors.

The royal compound had to be at least twice the size of the palace in Monteverre and it was filled with a history that fascinated her. To her delight, her request for a few books on the history of Zayyar led to her being introduced to an entire wing of the palace filled with the royal collections of art, sculptures and, best of all, books. Thousands and thousands of books.

Still, she spent the afternoon looking over her shoulder, expecting to find him standing in a doorway or walking towards her with that dark unreadable gaze. Not that she was waiting for him, she told herself. Really, she was quite glad to have the time to adjust to her new surroundings without feeling as if he was scrutinising her every move. She dined alone in her suite, a simple meal of traditional slow-cooked meats and fragrant rice. Afterwards she took an idle stroll down the corridor towards the Sheikh's wing, casually slowing as she passed the large gilded double doors.

'His Highness has gone to Valar for meetings,' her bodyguard said quietly.

'Of course.' She nodded, as though she knew exactly where her husband was and what he was doing. 'I thought this was the way to the garden terrace.' When she was kindly redirected to her destination she spent barely a moment looking around the exotic plants before returning to her room, feeling utterly foolish for leaving in the first place.

Valar was the new city on the coast; she had read about it in her studies. It was where her ball was to be held at the beginning of next month. She felt her mild irritation grow into a more solid simmering displeasure at her new husband's disappearing act. Was it so unrealistic to expect a single conversation with one's husband? She set to practising in her mind what she would say when she eventually saw him.

The next day passed in exactly the same fashion; meals were taken alone in her suite, except for a pleasant mid-morning tea with Nia. Aside from that, the only company she had were the various people in the Sheikh's employ, all of whom called her 'Your Highness' and did not make eye contact. Still, she took it in her stride, taking advantage of the pool of knowledge at her fingertips in the library and enjoying the heat of the sun on her face on a leisurely walk in the gardens.

After only two full days at the palace, she found herself longing for the calm of the evening when she could close the door of her private apartment and be completely alone. There were guards outside and a maid came to check in occasionally but, for the most part, she was left to her own devices. So far, that meant immediately changing into her pyjamas and camping out by the open balcony doors to read the books she had found on Zayyar's fascinating history and traditions. Occasionally she would look up and catch sight of the sprawling desert laid out beyond the palace walls, further than the eye could see. It took her breath away every time, the raw beauty of this place and how completely untouched it was. She had not expected to feel so calmed by the desert, or so drawn to it.

Her current reading material consisted mainly of books on the history of Zayyar and its customs but she had also taken time to learn the language of her new home outside the formal tutor-led lessons. She had always enjoyed exploring a new language on her own terms, finding the true rhythm of it by herself. As Sheikha, she would be expected to be knowledgeable and respectful of her nation's traditions but she did not necessarily have to become fluent in their language. She simply could not resist the idea of an entirely new tongue to perfect and actually have the chance to use it on a daily basis. It was something to keep her mind busy, she told herself, as her husband seemed to have zero interest in her company.

Despite her best attempts to fill her time, she felt loneliness begin to set in. She had always been comfortable with her own company, but suddenly being alone with her books didn't feel the same. Perhaps it was the fact that she was in a new country, in a new routine and surrounded by people who barely spoke to her. It was as though she had stepped into a glass cage surrounded by people. She was alone.

Her mobile phone seemed strangely unable to pick up a signal since they had touched down in Zayyar. It felt like a lifetime ago since she had stepped off the jet in the heart of the desert, but in reality it had only been three days. She was by no means a techno junkie but still, it was very isolating not being able to just pick up her phone and send an email or call one of her sisters on the odd occasion. After a few minutes investigating, she discovered it was most likely that the number was no longer in service. Probably, her father had cancelled it, a passive aggressive punishment for disobeying his orders to return to Monteverre for the engagement announcement. She presumed he knew by now that she had eloped with the Sheikh, rather than follow his plan for a grand wedding. That would have been a sight to behold.

It was no big deal; surely she could simply ask Khal's team what the protocol was for obtaining a new phone? A small laugh escaped her throat at the realisation that she was the Queen of an entire kingdom and she couldn't even obtain her own phone without permission. The restlessness that had plagued her all day intensified and she stood, stretching the muscles in her back and looking towards the clock on her bedside table to check the time. It was almost midnight, local time.

She calculated the time zones for a moment. Last she had heard, her sister Olivia was in New York. It was still a semi-reasonable hour there… She hadn't spoken to Olivia at all since recent events had begun to transpire. There simply hadn't been an opportunity. Unable to resist, she took a quick peek into the corridor outside her apartments and bit her lip as she found it deserted. Perhaps the guards switched shifts at midnight. She knew there was a phone in the small office beside the library. She could wait for permission…or she could just go. She was an adult, after all.

Not able to shake the sensation that she was a naughty teenager breaking the rules, she set off quickly for fear she might change her mind. Heart beating fast, she moved soundlessly in her bare feet, so eager she made a few wrong turns and wound up hopelessly lost. She cursed her own sense of direction, wishing she had paid more attention to the corridors in daylight. Still, it was a rather nice change from the monotony of the past few days. She actually felt a little bit free, wandering unchaperoned in the semi-darkness.

By the time she found her way back to the library, she had a little bounce in her step. She had forgotten what it felt like to walk around without guards following her every move like shadows. Even in university, she had been free to move about the campus by herself for most of the time.

Disappointment coursed through her when Olivia's phone number also turned out to be cancelled. Not wanting to waste her time alone, she turned on the computer on the desk. It had always been occupied by a guard on her previous visits to the library. Miraculously, she found the option for guest mode with a decent Internet connection and hurriedly set about signing into her email server. To her surprise, her inbox was flooded with concern from some of the members of her research team at university. With horror, she realised she had never said goodbye before unenrolling from her courses.

She made quick work of finding the number of the head of her research team in London and breathed a sigh of relief when he answered on the first ring. He brushed off her hurried apology at the late hour and seemed genuinely relieved to hear that she was well. He told her of the rest of the team's efforts to get in contact with her; naturally, all of their enquiries to the palace in Monteverre had been met with silence.

After a few minutes she learned that the team was coping quite well in her absence; it seemed she wasn't quite as indispensable as she had believed. She ended the call with a fond farewell, promising to try to arrange a trip to London in the future, although deep down she knew that if she did return it would be so far in the future that they would probably have all moved on further in their careers and forgotten her completely.

She turned to exit the office, stopping with a squeak at a looming figure leaning against the doorway.

'Thought you were all alone?' Khal drawled.

She was just as beautiful in her pyjamas as she had been in her wedding dress. That was Khal's first thought upon finding Cressida sneaking gracefully through the library in semi-darkness. It had been late when he'd returned to the palace so he had opted to wait until morning to alert his new bride to his presence. He had been sitting in a corner alcove, taking in the mountains of books she had been studying, when she'd entered, oblivious to his presence. He'd had every intention of leaving to allow her to complete her phone call in private... Until he'd realised the person she was speaking to in such hushed tones was another man. He had found his fists clenched tight as he'd stalked soundlessly closer to the office doorway.

'You startled me,' she breathed. 'I didn't know you had returned.'

'Do you usually wait until the middle of the night to call your friends?' he asked calmly, ignoring the knot of tension in his abdomen.

Her eyes widened slightly at his tone. 'I never said goodbye to some friends in London. I was just checking in…with my research team.'

'You are the Sheikha of Zayyar.' His voice clipped each word out like a gunshot.

Cressida's eyes widened with surprise. 'I am quite aware of my own title by now, thank you,' she said tightly. 'You sound angry. Why do I feel like I'm being scolded when I have not done anything wrong?'

'Perhaps you mistake anger for simple confusion as to why I just walked in on my wife having a hushed midnight conversation with an unknown man.'

'I will not be told who I can or cannot speak to. Especially when I have been here for days without anyone to speak to at all.'

Khal was silent for a moment, his jaw tight. 'This man. He is a close friend?'

'I've known him a few years through my work at the university,' she said. 'But no. I don't have many friends.'

Silence fell between them and Khal saw a flash of sadness in her eyes before she quickly turned her face from him.

'If that's all you want to ask, I've got an early start in the morning.' She took a couple of steps towards the door.

Khal moved sideways to block her way. 'Being Sheikha is a full-time job, Cressida,' he said, noting the way she tilted her stubborn chin upwards in answer to his tone. 'I need to know that you are prepared for the responsibilities of this life.'

'I've been feeling a little isolated so I made a phone call. I suppose I did miss my old life for a moment.' She half laughed. 'I always felt such happiness in the corner of my small apartment, working at my computer or reading. It keeps my mind working. Makes me feel like I'm achieving something, maybe. But anyway, I needn't have bothered because it seems my departure has not left any lasting impression.'

A faraway look crossed her delicate features, the barest sheen of moisture seeming to brighten her eyes for a split second before she hastily blinked it away. She took a deep breath, pinning him with a brave smile. 'I'm hardly planning to give up and run away after one difficult week.'

He took a step towards her. 'I'm sorry that you felt isolated here. I did not mean to...'

'To leave me completely alone in a new country less than twelve hours after our wedding?' she finished helpfully.

Khal winced, knowing her words were entirely true. He had abandoned her to his staff, believing she would find comfort enough in a busy routine while he dealt with the aftermath of the investigations into the tent fire, among other things. Perhaps there was also a small part of him that wished to put some distance between them after the familiarity of their wedding night. She was his wife. It was only natural he would feel some level of protectiveness towards her. The memory of the kiss they had shared in his suite after the fire had plagued him, sending him to bed each night in a sweat, sleep the furthest thing from his mind.

Almost as though she heard his thoughts, her tongue darted out to moisten her lips, leaving a glistening sheen along the plump pink flesh. He felt his body react instantly, heat rushing downwards. Clenching his fist, he cleared his throat. 'I have not been very attentive so far, it seems.'

'No, you have not,' she agreed, moving past him in the doorway to walk into the library beyond. 'But I understand that you had sudden matters to address that could not be ignored. Have you any update on what caused the fire in the encampment?'

Khal pursed his lips, trying and failing not to notice the gentle sway of her hips in her loose-fitting pyjama bottoms. 'It has been deemed accidental. I was just informed this afternoon, in fact.' He watched as her face visibly relaxed; she had been worried about the fire then. Of course she had.

He wished that the news had given him the same relief. The fact that his security team and the police had no idea who had been behind it and had no leads was frustrating. But he could not think of it now, not when she so clearly needed reassuring.

'You enjoy reading books about Zayyar,' he said, changing the subject, gesturing to where he had found her little nook in the corner.

She smiled, walking over to straighten the small mountain of books with an almost lover-like caress. 'It's a beautiful kingdom.'

'You weren't lying when you said that you consider reading a sport. I'd bet you've made your way through a quarter of my collection already.'

She blushed, turning away as she flicked idly through a volume on Zayyari etiquette and traditions. 'I suppose I just like to feel prepared in a new situation. To arm myself with as much knowledge as possible when I'm feeling out of my depth.'

Of course she was feeling overwhelmed. He had rushed ahead with their wedding without a second thought, put her life at risk in the encampment and then abandoned her at the first opportunity. As far as husbands went, he was already a spectacular failure.

'That is to be expected. Not many people would be quite so composed in the face of such upheaval in their normal routine.' He met her eyes. 'You may brush off my compliment but know that I mean it earnestly. And I would like to make this transition as easy as possible for you as you find your feet here. Starting with your own personal phone line in your suite, perhaps?'

'Thank you. That's very kind.' She smiled. 'My father had my mobile phone account cancelled at some point since we eloped.'

'King Fabian is not known for making direct statements when he is displeased.' Khal spoke thoughtfully. 'I will also have a top-of-the-range device delivered to your suite tomorrow.'

'Really, a simple landline is fine,' she argued.

'You are the Sheikha of Zayyar now, Cressida. If you want something, anything at all, it will be obtained for you. You need only ask.'

For a moment, he thought she might argue. He watched the delicate play of emotions cross her features as she bent to retrieve a book from the pile at their feet. When she stood up straight again, her face was a polite mask of control. Something inside him briefly wondered what lay underneath that mask, what she was truly feeling about her situation, but he brushed away the sentimental thought.

He escorted her back to her suite, making idle conversation about the various parts of the palace she had seen in his absence. As he listened to her genuine appreciation of his ancestral home, he found himself inwardly making plans to show her the hidden gems that few knew about. To play tour guide in his own kingdom and show her the true Zayyar.

He simply wanted her to feel at home here, he told himself, but a strange sensation seemed to envelope him in her presence. The physical attraction was there, of course, but something else had joined it. He wanted her to feel at ease with him, he realised.

After he bade her goodnight at her door and returned to his own adjoining suite, he sat at his desk and idly shuffled through official papers. His mind was not with his work tonight, nor had it been for the entire day. He had been eager to return to the palace almost from the moment he had left it. The chemistry between himself and his new bride was an unwelcome complication and until now he had not known how to manage it, except to keep a distance between them. But perhaps all he needed was a simple redirection. It was not weak or emotional to wish for an accord with the woman who would stand by his side for the next five years. It was practical and far more realistic than his original plan.

Humming to himself, he made a neat, concise list of plans and felt the dark mood that had plagued him begin to lift. Everything was still perfectly in order.

Cressida dreamt of her father, his face contorted with anger as he shouted down at her. She was small in the dream, afraid to speak but feeling his words pierce holes in her delicate skin. She woke with her throat parched dry as though she had been screaming. Dawn had just begun to break over the city; she could see the first flickers of pink light spreading out over the desert in the distance.

She took pleasure in dressing herself without an audience, much to the confusion of her maids, who entered her sitting room to find her fully clothed in one of the loose silk kaftans that had been provided as part of her new wardrobe. The material was a jade-green chiffon with satin lining, decorated with sparkling beads and tiny stones around the collar and cuffs. She had showered and allowed her long ash-blonde hair to dry naturally so it wasn't quite straight but still fell in pleasing waves down her back.

When she entered the dining room of the royal apartment she was surprised to find Khal already seated. He stood while she took her seat at the opposite end of the table, offering a pleasant good morning before returning to his coffee and newspaper. She ate quietly, glancing up every now and then to watch with fascination as he switched between his tablet computer and the broadsheet spread out across the table by his side. Taking notes, by the looks of it, she mused. It should not surprise her that his working day would begin the moment he opened his eyes.

When she had finished eating, he was still absorbed in his reading so she stood up quietly, intending to leave him in peace.

'My apologies for being so distracted; I'm not used to sharing breakfast with anyone.' Khal stood, neatly folding his paper and folding up the cover of his device before tucking it under his arm.

'There's no need for you to change your morning

rituals simply because I am here,' Cressida said earnestly. 'I have a morning packed full of lessons and dress fittings and goodness knows what else. I'm kept quite busy around here.'

'Yes, that's what I wanted to talk to you about. My advisors told me that so far you have been using the main library for all of your studies.'

'The library is wonderful. I'm happy to continue there.'

'I wanted to show you something, before you start your day.' He motioned for her to follow him out of the main door of the apartment, a strange lightness in his usually austere expression. 'It's just something I thought of after our conversation last night.'

Cressida kept her expression neutral as she followed him down the halls of the royal wing of the palace in the direction of the Sheikh's formal offices and library. She had been given a tour of this area of the palace but told that it was for official use only.

'This is my office and official rooms through here,' he said idly, gesturing to a door that led onto a room as big as a basketball court. She had not been permitted inside, but she had been told that many more rooms spread out from there, a library, secretarial offices and such. The Sheikh walked across the large sunny vestibule to a door tucked away at the end of the hallway. He hesitated for a moment before pushing it open and allowing her to enter first.

At first she wasn't quite sure if it was an office or a library. Books lined three of the four walls but there was also a working area on one side with a large cherrywood desk, complete with a computer, phone and pens. A long plush sofa occupied the other side of the room, facing a large arched window that overlooked the gardens beyond.

'I decided you needed a place of your own for your studies,' Khal said matter-of-factly. 'It used to be my office when I was the Crown Prince.'

Cressida walked over to one of the bookcases and ran her fingers along the spines. A place of her own. Her own little sanctuary. She had made one comment to him about missing her tiny study space back in London and he had gone and given her an entire office of her own. She darted a look over her shoulder to see him still standing in the doorway, watching her with hooded brows.

'You can have it redecorated to your own personal taste, of course. I won't be offended if you don't like the décor. And I will arrange to have whichever books you prefer transported here from the main library if the selection here is lacking—'

'It's perfect.' Her voice sounded surprisingly calm, in contrast to the alarming burst of emotion swelling in her chest. 'Thank you.'

He waved off her gratitude good-naturedly before glancing at the watch on his wrist. 'I must start my working day officially, but feel free to stay here and settle in if you wish. If you need anything at all, there is an intercom on the desk and an assistant assigned to you.'

'An assistant?' Cressida gasped.

'The Sheikha always has a personal assistant once royal duties commence,' he replied easily, as though it should have been obvious to her. 'You have three weeks until you officially enter into public life. The calendar of a Sheikha can be quite demanding.'

They were interrupted by two palace officials, seeking the Sheikh's urgent attendance in his office. Cressida motioned for him to go, thanking him once more before he disappeared through the door and closed it behind him with a gentle click.

She wandered over to the desk and sat slowly into the buttery soft leather swivel chair behind it. He had thought of her. He had put thought into her comfort beyond what was necessary. It was a strange feeling, having someone else looking out for her.

Placing both hands on the wood, she glanced down and smiled as she noticed the slim mobile handset that had been placed on top of a sheaf of papers. She lifted it, finding it had already been pre-programmed for her ease of use. She sighed with pleasure, hardly knowing where she would begin with all these wonderful gifts. She wondered if he even considered them gifts.

A wind blew gently through the open window, shuffling some of the papers across the desk. She gathered them back, noticing for the first time that they were stamped with the royal Zayyari crest on top in their signature wine and gold leaf design. But when she noticed the signature underneath, her breath caught completely. A feeling strangely like pride filled her chest as she ran her fingers over the ornate lettering, feeling the weight of the words press much further than just her fingertips.

From the desk of Her Royal Highness,
Sheikha Cressida Al Rhas of Zayyar

CHAPTER SEVEN

KHAL MADE A point of eating with Cressida each morning, inwardly congratulating himself as he noticed her mood lightening with each passing day. He told himself that it was simply in his best interests to ensure that she was comfortable at the palace, but truthfully he looked forward to their morning conversations. Soon, he began to forget to take his usual notes from the political broadsheets, abandoning the task to one of his secretaries in favour of occupying his time hearing about Cressida's progress in her studies. She showed a remarkable aptitude for retaining information, relaying some of her difficulties with the Zayyari language with humour and a total lack of self-consciousness.

On the rare evenings that he did not have meetings or functions to attend, they dined together in the apartment. It was far from an effort to keep his mind focused on the conversations that flowed with surprising ease between them; he enjoyed the new perspective of seeing his beloved kingdom and all of its traditions through her eyes. But still, beneath the iron of his control he fought the urge to let his gaze wander over her tempting curves or to linger when he bid her goodnight at the door to her room.

It seemed that married life made the time pass quickly and he found himself thinking less of his investigations into the fire at the encampment or his suspicions about who might have started it. Exactly two weeks had passed since their wedding when Khal found his good mood completely thrown off course by a single piece of information let slip by one of his secretaries. He called for his Chief of Security immediately, sitting behind his desk with clenched fists as he waited for Sayyid to arrive.

'You wished to see me, Your Highness?' Sayyid entered, a heavy look in his eyes.

'Close the door.' Khal spoke slowly, taking every ounce of his effort to control the temper that threatened to spill over at any moment. He gestured for the other man to take a seat before he stood and paced to the other side of his desk.

'Is there a problem, Sire?'

'One might say that, yes,' Khal gritted. 'If you would describe finding out that there has been yet another incident a *problem.*'

'If you mean the small situation that was contained last week...'

'I will decide what situation is considered small,' Khal growled. 'What makes you believe that your King should not be informed of any kind of threat in his own kingdom? That I should find out a week after the fact that there was an intruder apprehended in the middle of the night, scaling the palace walls?'

'With the utmost respect, Sire, there have been instances of people trying to climb the palace walls in the past. The man did not breach the security fences and did not carry any weaponry; therefore it was classed as a non-dangerous incident.'

'Was he questioned? Did he have ties to any rebellious factions?' Khal felt pressure build in his temples as he noticed Sayyid's mouth tighten.

'We questioned him and ascertained that he was a youth on a foolish dare. Even Lazarov agreed that it was best not to make an incident of something so mundane.'

'Roman was informed of this incident, was he?' Khal fought the annoyance that rose in his chest at the mention of his friend's name. Roman's security firm had trained the entire palace guard; of course they would go to him if there had been an attempted breach. No one dealt with high profile risk assessment and security better than The Lazarus Group. Khal had called upon Roman himself within hours of the fire in the encampment. It had been Roman who had informed him that the private investigation had been classed as one hundred per cent accidental, with no sinister or deliberate intention.

In that same phone call his friend's tone had become concerned as he had reminded Khal of instances in the past where his need for heightened security had been extreme. Of how he needed to trust his team to do their job and stop looking for threats where none existed.

Khal felt anger rise within him once more as he heard that same tone of concern in Sayyid's voice.

'Sire, I can assure you that the Sheikha is safe—'

'I have not mentioned the Sheikha once,' Khal fumed. 'This is about your complete insubordination in not reporting a potentially dangerous matter to your King.'

Sayyid stood suddenly, open defiance on his face.

'There was no danger; that is what I am trying to make you see. What many have tried to make you see.'

Khal turned and took a few steps away, feeling the anger within him reach its peak. Truthfully, perhaps he'd been thinking of Cressida's safety when he'd imagined the unknown intruder scaling the walls in the dead of night. But this was not just about possible danger to his wife. This was about Zayyar.

His father had always made a point of reminding him how quickly rebellion could resurge when one rested in a state of peace. It was his duty to ensure his staff did not take that peace for granted and make mistakes. He inhaled deeply, his jaw pulsing with the effort of keeping his tone measured. Of keeping his control. 'You will take a leave of absence from your duties to account for this error in judgement. One week, effective immediately.'

Sayyid's eyes narrowed. For a moment Khal wondered if the line was about to be crossed. If the other man would openly defy his King's orders.

'As you wish, Your Highness. I'll make the arrangements,' Sayyid finally said. He bowed low before turning and exiting the room without another word.

Khal paced the floor of his study for what felt like hours in the aftermath of the confrontation with his trusted employee, feeling the pressure in his head pulse and thrum with every step. He sat down in a high-backed armchair, resisting the urge to fling the nearby coffee table across the room. He would not allow his staff to decide what he could and would not be told. He had the right to know everything that happened within his own palace. Roman's calm voice popped into his head once more. Was this one of those situations he'd referred to? Was he seeing danger where it did not exist? Should he simply trust his security team to do their job and stop trying to control every single thing in his orbit? He did kick out in frustration then, his foot making hard contact with the heavy marble leg of the coffee table in front of him.

'Having a tantrum?'

A quiet voice shook him from his brooding; he silently hoped it was not Cressida but at the same time knew that it was. She stood a few feet away, wrapped in a pale pink silk robe. He leaned his head back, allowing himself a moment to take her in before he spoke. 'Sheikhs do not have tantrums. We have momentary losses of composure.'

'Ah.' She hovered nervously in the doorway. 'I came back down to get a book and I saw your light still on. Am I interrupting?'

'Come in. Though I might not be the best company.'

He stood up, taking a long languorous stretch and covertly watching as her gaze rose to follow his movements before darting away. Khal felt the beginning of a smile tease his lips. It dawned on him that this was the first time she had set foot inside his office.

Her eyes wandered to his desk, where a handful of professional photographs of their wedding ceremony were scattered. Khal had just received them that morning and hadn't quite decided what to do with them yet. She moved closer, her fingertips trailing over the images delicately.

'I look…completely different,' she said in that same quiet voice. Her brow was furrowed as she picked up a shot of them both with their foreheads touching.

'You don't like them?' he asked, genuinely eager to know the answer.

'They are very well done.' She smiled.

'That is not what I asked.'

'I suppose they're quite convincing. Romantic and dreamy. But when one knows the truth, the illusion is spoiled a little.' She placed the photo back down and arranged the others in a square formation, avoiding his gaze. 'It's a strange feeling, being married but not actually being married, isn't it?'

'We are married,' he said with a hint of irony. 'I have photographic evidence.'

'You know what I mean—we have this arrangement.' Cressida sighed, moving over to inspect the collection of tiny ships in bottles that adorned the shelves of his study. 'I never understood how they got such detailed works inside these things without breaking it,' she said absentmindedly, running a fingertip along the glass that encased a large rare Marlin.

'It's a hobby of mine,' he said idly, wondering why her comment about not actually being married stuck in his mind.

'You made all these?' Her eyes widened as she took in the wall of shelves. 'How on earth do you find the time?'

'It calms my mind.' He shrugged, not quite sure why he'd shared something so personal. A king did not struggle with an overactive mind. A king had complete control over his thoughts at all times.

'It looks incredibly complicated.' She was still peering at various models, genuine appreciation on her features.

'It's simple enough once you approach it from a point

of logic. My father introduced me to it at a young age.'
A smile teased the corner of his lips as he remembered
some of the tantrums he had thrown when he'd continued to fail at lifting the mast of the tiny ship. His father
had always remained seated, never raising a hand or losing his temper. 'Go over your plan and begin again,' he
would say calmly. Now, as a grown man, he could see
that his father had given him the tools to harness the
anger and uncontrolled nature that he had shown even
as a young boy. There was no place in Zayyar's future
for another king without self-control. For another king
ruled by his own selfish desires.

'I was just about to order some tea,' he said brusquely,
walking away from her to gather his thoughts for a moment. 'You are welcome to join me.' He kept his tone
light, telling himself he was inviting her to stay because
he was simply not in the mood to be alone with his own
thoughts. She was a good conversationalist. He had no
ulterior motives for wanting to be alone with his wife
in his study at night...

Clearly, she was having a similar thought process,
considering she took a full two minutes to come to a
decision before lowering herself into the armchair opposite his own. He had not been lying; he had been about
to order tea. It was the only thing that calmed him in a
mood such as this one.

His staff were efficient, laying out the perfectly pol-
ished pots and utensils between them, hot steam rising
from the ornate copper teapot.

To his surprise, Cressida began the service, perform-
ing the Zayyari ritual with seemingly effortless movements. It was only because he studied her so closely that
he noticed the slight tremble of her fingers, or the way

her brow creased momentarily as she focused on her performance. He reached out to accept his cup from her fingers, deliberately brushing his thumb across her skin.

'And you say that you do not feel like you are truly married?' He sat back, savouring the taste of the sweet traditional brew on his tongue. 'This seems like very wifely behaviour to me.'

'Well, you would know more about that than I do.' She focused on stirring her tea, taking a moment to realise what she had said. 'Oh, I'm sorry. I'm so thoughtless…'

'Don't apologise.' Khal shook off the comment, but still he found himself fighting the sudden sharp jab of discomfort with the reference to his first marriage. Perhaps because, since they'd sat down, he had been acutely distracted by the woman who sat across from him. Or maybe it was because his ring now lay upon her finger and so to think of another time seemed inappropriate somehow. Truthfully, he'd thought of his first wife less and less as the years passed. And, even then, only to ponder a new lead in his investigations into her accident. It had been five years, after all. He knew he could not feel the same intense emotions for ever, but still it brought guilt to realise he had truly accepted her death and moved on.

'It seems morbid to ask if you sat like this in the past.' Cressida spoke softly. 'You have never spoken of your first marriage. I'll admit that I am curious.'

'My first marriage was very different for many reasons,' Khal said simply, taking another sip of his tea. 'I was very different.'

'Your sister told me that you grieved for a long time. I got the impression that you were both very much in love.' She met his eyes, a strangely guarded expression on her usually open features.

'We were.' He flexed the tightness from his fingers, laying his palm down flat on the arm of the chair. 'In the beginning, at least.'

'Oh.'

One syllable was all she needed to portray that she understood. She did not push the subject further and for that he was grateful. It was only the beginning of the myriad secrets of his seemingly perfect marriage to Priya. He had never spoken to anyone of the fact that all was not as it seemed. But now he felt strangely lighter having spoken of it, never having considered that there might be weight to carrying secrets.

'My parents' marriage was arranged,' Cressida said after a while. 'My grandmother always said they were lucky to have fallen madly in love as a result.' She pursed her lips, meeting his eyes for a moment before looking away. 'Seeing what falling out of love has done to them, I have always been of the opinion that it was better to have a marriage free of emotions.'

Khal frowned at her admission, picturing King Fabian and his cold, uninterested wife. He had been in their company on a number of occasions, and each time he had become more aware of the deep well of problems in the royal marriage. He was of the opinion that the issues ran far deeper than simply falling out of love, but he kept that thought to himself.

'Is that why you agreed to marry me?' he asked. 'Other than your extreme devotion to your kingdom, of course.'

Cressida seemed to shift in her seat slightly, one hand

adjusting the material of her nightgown. 'I had many reasons for accepting this…arrangement.'

'This is a marriage, *habibti.* Make no mistake.' He did not mean for the hardness to creep into his voice but all of a sudden the idea that she saw their union as some kind of cold business arrangement was not palatable to him, for reasons unknown. After all, political marriages such as theirs were essentially built on business, were they not?

'I'm not saying that we each aren't bound by the same rules as usual marriages,' she said hurriedly. 'I just mean that, behind closed doors, we both know different.'

'Do you feel bound by the rules, Cressida?' he said silkily, feeling a pang of irritation at the feelings her words evoked. The memory of a similar conversation in the past came to the surface, another woman's voice.

'I have never been good at playing by the rules, Khal. I'm sorry.'

'I have no desire to enter into a verbal sparring match at midnight,' Cressida said, standing up and shaking out the fabric of her nightgown. 'You were clearly aggravated by something before I came in here and I think it's best that I say goodnight.'

'Oh, no, you don't.' Khal stood, moving so that he blocked her way. 'You see, I like to finish conversations, not walk away from them if they get a little uncomfortable.'

'I don't feel like this is a conversation any longer. I feel like you are putting words into my mouth.'

She'd mentioned her mouth and, sure enough, that was where his eyes wandered, the perfect pink flesh teasing him. 'Do you feel bound by the rules of this marriage?' he asked again, softer this time. The air between them thrummed with awareness.

'Sometimes.' She half whispered the word, her breath seeming slightly laboured all of a sudden. 'But perhaps not quite in the way that you think.'

'Do you feel unhappy here with me, Cressida?' he asked, feeling the sizzle of something dangerous in the air between them. He wanted to know the answer to his question, the honest answer. To allow him to see beneath the facade she always wore around him.

He wanted something real.

Cressida shook her head once, her eyes meeting his. 'I don't feel unhappy when I'm with you. I feel...frustrated.'

He wasn't sure who leaned in first, but suddenly their mouths were locked and it was like the first drink after weeks in the desert. He feasted on her, taking every ounce of the longing that he could feel in her kiss and giving back in equal measure. He felt the weight of her arms around his neck, her chest pressed tightly against his, and yet it still wasn't enough. He pressed her back against the bookcase, ignoring her sharp intake of breath as he raised her arms above her head and began a slow trail down her neck.

Her groans sent the blood rushing straight to his groin, not that he hadn't already lost control of that particular piece of his anatomy. She moved against him, consciously or unconsciously coming into contact with his arousal and giving a slight gasp. Khal looked down into her widened eyes, tension furling and unfurling in his lower abdomen.

'Tell me to stop,' he commanded. 'Tell me that you don't want this.'

'I can't,' she whispered, lowering her face into the curve of his neck and pressing a hot kiss to his skin. 'I think I have wanted this from the first moment I saw you.'

The kiss undid him completely, along with the words. He waited a moment as she kissed along his clavicle, running her hot tongue along his skin. Unable to cope with the torture of standing still, he ran his hands over her shoulders, gently spreading the delicate vee of her robe wide enough to lower the neck of her nightgown and expose the porcelain skin of one breast. He let his hands explore one hardened peak until she leaned her head back in sensual abandon. Then he leaned down to replace fingers with lips and tongue. He thoroughly pleasured one delicate breast before moving on to afford the same attentions to its twin. Each movement of his tongue brought forth groans of pleasure, which Cressida tried to stifle with her fist. They were in his study, after all.

She moved against him again, more impatiently this time, as though she knew exactly what she wanted. Her pelvis fitted in line with his so perfectly. It would be so easy to just wrap her legs around his waist and slide himself inside her. He would take her rough and hard, sliding in and out of her moist heat until neither of them could remember their own name…

'Don't stop, Khal.' Her hushed plea threatened to undo him. 'Please.'

Spurred on by the raw need in her voice, he continued his explorations, removing her robe and letting his fingers gather her nightgown up until it bunched just under her hips. Pinning the fabric with one hand, he found the lace-covered centre of her and applied a gentle pressure.

* * *

Cressida's attempts to remain quiet were short-lived; soon her loud gasps and stifled moans filled the room. She had never felt such unbearable pleasure as she did with his hands on her, touching her. It was as though he knew exactly how she liked it, exactly how she touched herself in the dark of night when no one was watching. Khal let out a deeply male groan of pleasure as she moved herself against his hand, wanting more than he gave.

He pulled the lace down over her hips, watching her eyes the whole time. Perhaps he was waiting to see if she had finally come to her senses and decided she didn't want this, after all. She did not falter. She had made her decision the moment he stood in front of her, all male sexual energy. Perhaps tomorrow she would remember why this was such a bad idea but in this moment she had never wanted anything more in her life.

She became impatient with his slow movements and kicked the material off the rest of the way, enticing a husky laugh from his throat. She smiled, amazed that this felt so right all of a sudden when moments ago they had been talking about practicality. There was nothing practical about what they were doing right now and they both knew it.

His fingers came into contact with her bare flesh and within seconds she could feel her body begin to pulse and tighten as it began to ascend towards climax. He must have sensed it too because, just as she had almost reached the peak, he stopped.

'What are you—' Her stunned words were stifled by his kiss as he gathered her up into his arms and carried her a few steps across the room to a long sofa. The cushions were soft underneath her but the fabric of her nightgown bunched uncomfortably around her waist.

As though he read her mind, he helped her to be rid of the pesky layers. All of a sudden she was completely naked, spread out before him while he was still completely clothed. He paused for a moment, eyes darkening with pleasure as he drank her in, then he set about removing his own clothing. By the time he was completely naked, Cressida's throat had gone dry. He was... magnificent. There was no other way to describe the hard expanse of copper-toned skin on show. He was well built in a suit but nude, he was powerful. Muscles rippled along a trim abdomen, leading to trim hips and... She gulped, wondering how on earth that was going to fit anywhere belonging to her.

'I have dreamed of doing this,' he murmured, moving over her so that their bodies were entwined. She could feel the heat of him pressing between her thighs, her own excitement slightly embarrassing now that no clothing was between them.

She was nervous but definitely ready. As he poised himself over her, she was struck by the weight of this moment. He moved against her with such slowness, she felt a lump in her throat. She could feel his hard heat as he slid the first inch inside; there was only slight pain as he moved further, stretching her to accommodate him. His eyes widened for a moment as some of her discomfort must have showed on her face. He made to pull away but Cressida gripped his hips with her thighs, holding him tightly against her. Keeping their bodies joined.

He uttered a curse under his breath, his breathing laboured as he gently pressed his forehead against hers, holding his body still with impressive control.

'Don't stop.' Cressida breathed. She arched herself against him and felt the join of their bodies pulse pleasurably. To her relief, he moved once more in response, then twice, placing one hand between them to slide his thumb against that part of her that drove her wild. What little pain there had been soon receded completely and only pleasure remained as her body quickly got the hang of what to do. She felt pleasure like nothing she had ever experienced building deep within her with every thrust. Her body seemed to move against him of its own volition and she noticed Khal hiss between his teeth.

'Oh, yes, *habibti*, just like that,' he practically growled as he spread her legs wider, moving even deeper, increasing his pace.

She felt him begin to lose control, his neck straining as his own climax approached. The sight of this powerful man at her mercy seemed to spur her on, bringing pleasure like she had never experienced crashing down upon her and sending her body into waves of absolute bliss. Cressida felt a moment of confusion as he pulled away from her at the last moment then bit her lower lip as she realised that he had only withdrawn just in time before his own climax hit him.

Khal fell back against the cushions of the sofa, head arched back in the pose of a man completely exhausted and satisfied. His chest rose and fell in a steady rhythm, the barest sheen of sweat glistening on his dark skin. Cressida could not look away, wanting to remember every detail of this perfect moment. She had never imagined that her first time would be quite so intimate and filled with passion.

Not only had she just made love for the first time, she had made love with her husband. The thought brought gooseflesh to her skin and she cursed herself for having such a sentimental reaction.

Truthfully, Cressida had absolutely no idea what one was supposed to say in this situation. Should she make small talk? Should she tell him that she had enjoyed it, they should do it again some time? It was insane, she had stood in front of a crowd and pledged her devotion to this man and he to her. The entire world now believed them to have had a secret love story worthy of movies and magazine spreads. And yet, in this moment, as the silence stretched onwards, she realised that they were just two people who had finally given in to a passion that neither of them quite understood.

Khal felt as though he had just run a marathon, but in the best way possible. He lay back on the sofa, eyes closed, but sleep was the furthest thing from his mind. He was avoiding the woman who lay alongside him, delaying the moment when he would have to confront the reality of what had just transpired between them.

First, he had not used any protection. Second, his wife had clearly been an innocent and he had crudely deflowered her on a sofa.

Suppressing the urge to growl at his own loss of control, he stood up and began to gather up their clothes.

There could not be a child. He could not bear the thought of history repeating itself… He paused for a long moment at his desk, his body seemingly frozen. He felt such an acute loss of control it was as though his thoughts swam away from him every time he tried to grasp them.

'Could you hand me my nightgown?' a quiet voice

came from the sofa. He turned, not knowing how long he had stood immobile and silent while she waited.

Guilt engulfed him as he saw the uncertainty on Cressida's features as she accepted the nightgown and hurriedly shielded her naked body from him.

'You were a virgin,' he said softly, sitting alongside her and turning her cheek so that she met his eyes. 'I would have taken more time, had I known. Made it better for you.'

'We didn't exactly plan for this, either of us.' She spoke with quiet sincerity. 'But it was quite pleasurable…for me, anyway.'

Khal looked down at the bare skin of her thighs, which had been wrapped around his waist mere minutes before. God, but he wanted her all over again. He exhaled a long breath, astounded at the complete deterioration of his adult mind to that of a lust-crazed youth.

Suddenly, Cressida stood up and pulled her arms through her nightgown, shielding her body from view. Khal fought the urge to pull her back down.

'I understand that you might be worried that this… that tonight would complicate matters between us.' She spoke with a strange coldness in her voice.

'Do you believe that it won't?' Khal asked. 'Tonight was irresponsible on my part, in more ways than one.'

She busied herself by pulling her hair back from her face, twisting it around itself in a neat trick that kept it secured atop her head with no clasps or ties. Next, she retrieved her robe, slipping her arms into it quickly.

Khal stood, quite aware that he had not yet bothered to put on his own clothing. He watched as she lowered her gaze for a split second before hurriedly looking away to focus on the wall behind his head as she spoke.

'We were both irresponsible. We are both adults. We got carried away tonight but we can simply agree that this need not happen again.'

'When I say irresponsible, I mean that I didn't use protection, Cressida.' Khal took a step towards her.

'That won't be an issue.' She straightened her shoulders, lifting her hand almost as a barrier between them. 'Presuming that you are...healthy?'

'Of course I am healthy,' he growled.

'Good. Well, I take medication to regulate my cycle,' she said matter-of-factly, tying the sash of her robe with an almost vicious precision. 'So it seems we have nothing else to worry about.'

She made to step away from him. Khal grabbed her by the wrist. 'Just like that? You've forgotten about what just happened in here?'

Her sharp intake of breath was loud in the silence of the night. 'We both agreed that this marriage was to remain free of complications.'

'And you immediately feel confident that you can go back to that plan?'

Cressida frowned. 'Did you not make it clear to me in the beginning that you were not seeking a true wife?'

Khal stepped back as though burned. 'Of course.'

'Then I think it's probably best for us to go back to our rooms...separately. Perhaps take some distance from each other over the next few days.'

'Yes, of course. Retreat and regroup,' Khal murmured, confused at his own irritation at her calm approach. He did not wish to have to dampen down the hopes of an overly sentimental virgin. He should be thanking his lucky stars at his good fortune. She nodded once, bidding him a very civilised goodnight before disappearing through the door of his office with seemingly effortless composure.

Khal waited until her footsteps had disappeared completely before leaving the office himself.

His feet seemed to know where to take him even before his brain registered where he was going. The open courtyards past the eastern wing of the palace led out onto a long tropical garden. Khal followed a marble path inset with aqua-blue stones that sparkled in the light of the full moon. The path sloped downhill to where a small stone fountain took precedence. It had been many years since he had come here. For a long time this had been his preferred place to sit and brood. Perhaps brooding was the wrong word to use—sorrow was the real emotion that one felt at this fountain.

A small marble square adorned the front of the fountain's stone facade. A single aquamarine stone glittered in the centre of the square. Khal placed his hand over the stone, feeling the warmth of it seep through his skin. He had chosen this spot because the sunshine was uninterrupted here during the day. At the time, that had seemed important. There was no name inscribed on the stone, no words to mark the sorrowful reason this fountain stood on this particular spot.

His son had never taken his first breath, and in Zayyari culture that meant that he had not existed. There was no grave. No tomb at which to kneel and pray.

But he had prayed.

He had prayed for the infant son he would never know, and for the wife who had changed for ever. Something had died inside him the day he had been told that Priya had lost their child. He had been on the other side of the world, and protocol had meant he was not able to return for days after. By the time he had finally reached her bedside, the woman looking back at him was not his Priya any longer. Her own death had come less than a year later.

He had not discussed with Cressida the reasons why he had no desire for an heir of his own. For those brief moments, imagining that she might carry his child had made his insides turn to stone. He'd told himself time after time that a leader did not show his fears. This was a half-truth—just because he did not show it, did not mean that he didn't harbour fears that ran deep into his soul.

CHAPTER EIGHT

CRESSIDA GASPED AS the helicopter swooped low to give them a panoramic view of the spectacular coastline of Valar. The city's skyline was impressive, dominated by silver and glass high-rise buildings and ornate hotels. Further down in the distance she could see the swimming pools of the beach-side resorts, tourists no more than tiny black dots on the white sand. They set down on top of a building so high Cressida felt every muscle in her body clench. Reminding herself not to look down, she was jolted when Khal's warmth slid closer to her on the leather seats as he spoke to the pilot, his voice barely audible over the roaring din of the chopper blades slowing to a stop.

She had barely seen him in the week that had passed since the night in his study. He did not eat breakfast with her, nor did he make any impromptu invitations to dine together in the evenings. She had missed the ease of their conversations but told herself it was for the best. He would never want a relationship with her beyond the sexual chemistry between them. A casual sexual relationship was simply not an option for a woman who was already married to the man in question. It would be utter madness to expect things to remain free of emotions, no strings attached.

She was escorted down from the helicopter by two of the security team but it was Khal who took her hand in his and guided her across the blustery rooftop to the lift. Once inside, she released a breath she hadn't realised she'd been holding and heard a rumble of quiet male laughter erupt alongside her.

'Did you fear I would allow you to fall off the rooftop?' he asked, his hand still holding hers captive within his own. He spoke idly, his gaze fixed on the numbers on the display panel as the lift came to a stop and the doors slid open to reveal a square windowless hallway.

'I'm glad you find my fear of heights entertaining,' she quipped, a reluctant smile crossing her own lips as she looked up into a pair of dark brown eyes filled with mirth.

As usual, part of the security detail had already performed a sweep in preparation for their arrival. They were escorted into a spacious foyer and promptly left alone.

All thoughts momentarily left her brain as she was greeted with the most spectacular view she had ever seen. The large open-plan space was sumptuously decorated in bright modern monochrome and sky-blue, but the main attraction was the double height wall of curved plate glass that offered an unobstructed view of the entire city skyline, beautifully framed by a glimpse of the Arabian Sea on one side. The window was so wide and so clear, it was as though the marble tiles simply ended on a precipice, leaving the viewer at the risk of toppling over the edge. It made her stomach tighten, but still she could appreciate the view.

'This city is…breathtaking…' Cressida murmured, still making sure that she remained firmly in the centre of the room.

'This city will soon be the future of Zayyar, thanks to you,' he said, warmth in his eyes. 'News of our marriage has already opened doors that once were firmly closed. Tonight's celebration will solidify many new connections for us.'

Cressida had already been told by her advisors of the progress that had been made since their marriage had become public knowledge. Tonight's formal celebration would bring politicians and foreign dignitaries from across the world here to show their support. However, there would not be a single member of her own family at the event. A fact that did not surprise her in the slightest. Her older sister, Eleanor, was on a charity mission in North Africa but had promised to come and visit soon, while her middle sister, Olivia, was busily setting up the headquarters of her literacy foundation in New York.

Her parents had openly refused the invitation, stating a scheduling conflict. They had half-heartedly organised an event to be held in Monteverre over the coming week and invited her and Khal for an official visit. A pathetic attempt at a show of power by her father, but still Cressida knew that his alliance was vital to Khal so she would dutifully attend.

She was to be on show to the world tonight for the first time as Sheikha. The thought terrified her almost as much as being up at this height did.

'Come and see the view. The window is bulletproof, shockproof—very safe, I assure you.' Khal moved to knock one hand against the glass pane.

Cressida raised one hand instinctively. 'There is *really* no need to demonstrate!'

A dimple appeared in the corner of his mouth again, that mischievous half smile that made her stomach flip. He braced one hand on the glass wall, shifting so that his weight leaned against it as he looked out into the distance. 'You get a much better view of the coastline over here than from all the way across the room. Just a suggestion.'

He was utterly mad; that was the only explanation for it. Who on earth could manage to look so serene and relaxed while seeming to hover on the edge of falling to their death?

'Is this your way of proving what a fearless leader you are? It's really not necessary.'

'I am simply trying to show you that you will not fall.' He spoke with surprising softness as he turned to face her. 'The danger exists only in your mind.'

In a few long strides he was beside her, taking her gently by the wrist. Her breath caught painfully in her throat at the heat of his skin on her own. She did not resist as he gently pulled her, step by torturous step, across the marble-tiled floor until she stood in the exact same spot as he had. He took her hand and placed her trembling palm against the cold glass. Cressida felt her insides tremble as she tried not to look down, focusing on the sensation of his hand still pinning her own in place.

'Open your eyes.' The command was gentle, but a command nonetheless. She gingerly fluttered one eyelid open, feeling as though her heart was about to beat straight out of her chest. He had not been lying when he said the view was better over here. On one side she could see the entire coastline stretching out into the distance, the sun sparkling on the water like a thousand diamonds. They were otherwise surrounded by a sea of sleek modern buildings and hotels, with the barest glimpse of unspoiled desert peeking out in the distance.

'Just don't look down.' Khal's voice came from somewhere near her ear as he removed his hand from hers and stood alongside her.

'You just reminded me that there is a down to look at.' She exhaled a little harder but resisted the urge to step back.

'Your composure is effortlessly regal, Your Highness.' She could hear the smirk in his voice as he placed one hand on the glass and faced away from her.

She couldn't help but let the corner of her own mouth turn up. 'I think all these brave masculine displays of royal window-leaning have reassured me.'

He turned to face her, a strange expression on his face. 'Now, you see, describing it as brave and masculine strokes my ego. Why lessen the effect by making it a royal activity?'

'I doubt most people would think that being royal lessens anything at all.'

'Ah, but we know better, don't we?' he said softly, his gaze travelling down her body for a split second. He swallowed, a frown creasing his brow.

The way he used the word 'we' so easily, she could almost imagine for a moment that they were a normal couple sharing a quiet moment of intimacy. She looked away, feeling the acute sting of awareness that she was looking for something that would never exist. Strange that, no matter what situation she was in, this feeling was always familiar, like an itchy blanket. The feeling of wanting more from someone but knowing she would never have it. Feeling as if she should be grateful for whatever small sliver of attention she had been given. The old pain threatened to overwhelm her until a silky voice invaded her reverie.

'Your mind has wandered away.'

Pulling herself back to the moment, she nodded, avoiding his gaze. 'I must be tired,' she offered, knowing she was lying but just wanting to retreat to her own space and analyse whatever she was feeling.

'You should rest, then. We leave for the ball at eight.'

Cressida nodded, making a mumbled show of thanks as he escorted her to her bedroom door before practically darting from his side. With the door firmly closed between them, she leaned back against the solid wood and waited for her heartbeat to return to normal.

Suddenly she longed for the solitude of the palace and the comfort of not being in such close proximity to the man who set her heartbeat racing and her stress levels rising. It was just simple chemical awareness, she told herself. He was the only man she had ever been close to, the only man who had ever kissed her or touched her. She had been married for less than a month. There was still another four years and eleven months to survive.

Unsurprisingly, she spent the following few hours in a less than restful state. As the sun began to dip in the evening sky, Cressida forced a smile as she took in her reflection in the floor-length mirror of her dressing room. The dress her team had chosen for the ball was a deliberately Western-styled design of midnight-blue lace, elegant and figure-hugging. If she could have chosen a gown to wear upon her first formal occasion as Queen, she could not have chosen one more perfect than this.

The silhouette made her appear more womanly, without making her feel self-conscious. The delicate capped sleeves were adorned with tiny seed pearls and the tiniest glints of sapphire. The same gems adorned her ears and her wrist, designed in Monteverre she was told, which was a nice touch. East meets West, she thought wryly as she gave a little turn in the mirror. She looked up, noticing that the door had opened, and was met with the dauntingly attractive sight of her husband in his formal robes. The King, she corrected herself sternly. The more she thought of him as her husband, the harder it was to forget what she wanted to forget. Taking a couple of breaths before she turned, she steeled herself for the onslaught of simply being in his presence. They were not alone in the room by any means, surrounded by the remnants of her wardrobe team, her assistant and members of her security detail. And yet she felt overheated and on edge.

'You look…beautiful,' he said, sincerity in the deep baritone of his voice.

'Thank you.' Cressida bowed her head slightly, clasping her hands in front of her. 'I thought we were meant to meet in the foyer?'

'I thought it best that I escort you down myself.' He extended his hand. 'That is, if that is all right with you?'

Cressida fought the urge to roll her eyes at the strained formality of it all. Instead, she straightened her spine and placed her hand in his.

Apart from a near miss when her heel got caught in the train of her dress coming down the stairs, their entrance to the ball was utterly flawless, as planned.

Cressida bowed and curtsied to various foreign dignitaries as needed, projecting what she hoped was an air of calm regal elegance when internally she felt far from it. Khal remained by her side as they were met with a queue of guests waiting for introductions to the new Queen of Zayyar.

As she'd expected, most of the guests commented on her appearance while choosing to compliment her husband on his most recent accomplishments. With her, they gushed over her designer jewellery and fawned over how utterly flawless her skin was. As though she had any control over the fact that her skin was pale and clear.

After a time, the smile she had pasted on her face began to hurt her cheeks so she simply stopped smiling. Apart from noticing Khal staring at her on a number of occasions, no one else seemed to notice. She was grateful when they sat down finally, having not eaten since breakfast in preparation for the event. Apparently it was customary to starve oneself before wearing a designer gown in order to achieve maximum leanness and avoid bloating. She had developed a new appreciation for what her sisters must have gone through in the past while she had avoided occasions such as this.

The menu was a mixture of traditional Zayyari meats and spices arranged in various European-style dishes. It was an ingenious incorporation of textures and flavours on the part of the Michelin star chefs who had been employed for the occasion. But, honestly, she could have been eating plain porridge and it would have tasted like sweet ambrosia.

'I see you have found your appetite.'

Cressida looked up, trying in vain to hide the gigantic mouthful of chicken she had just placed in her mouth. It was entirely impossible to appear ladylike or delicate when one's mouth was full of food. Khal smiled, stifling laughter with his hand as he leaned close.

'You will start a rumour that the King of Zayyar routinely starves his new bride.'

'I forgot to eat,' she said quickly, grabbing a napkin to dab the corners of her mouth. The man had barely spoken two words to her since escorting her into the banquet; of course he would choose now to begin a conversation. 'I had hoped nobody was looking.'

'I sincerely doubt that is the case. The entire gathering is captivated by you,' he said in a low voice, leaning in so that it seemed perhaps that they were having an intimate moment. 'You look…exceptionally regal this evening.'

Cressida felt a shiver run down her spine, having him so close, having his delicious scent invading her senses. The way he was looking at her, the depths of his dark eyes seeming to bore deep into her soul, she could not decide if he was continuing the show for the benefit of their guests or if perhaps he was feeling the same pull that she did, considering what had transpired between them a week ago. Or perhaps her hormones were simply not getting the message yet, she thought wryly.

Before he had a chance to dazzle her with any more of his flowery compliments, they were discreetly interrupted by one of Khal's assistants. A quick conversation passed in hushed tones before Khal turned back to her, a crease furrowing his brow.

'We are needed for a moment outside—nothing to worry about, just formalities.' He extended his hand to her, making quiet apologies to the handful of guests at their table before escorting her out through a set of double doors and into a sitting room of sorts.

There were a handful more assistants waiting for them, each of whom began talking in Zayyari so quickly that Cressida found it difficult to even catch a single word she recognised.

'English, please, for the benefit of your Queen,' Khal said briskly.

Cressida's eyes widened slightly at the tone he used. She had never heard him sound so impatient.

'There has been a report in the media…' one of the female assistants began, averting her eyes from Cressida's worried gaze as she spoke.

The chief of the team, a man with greying hair and beady eyes, moved from the side of the room, a large file in his hands. 'Your Highness, I apologise sincerely for disturbing your dinner, but protocol demands that you be alerted immediately to a report of this nature. When it is in the national interest.' He extended the black file to Khal, who took it immediately, opening it and scanning it.

Cressida felt the slight ball of tension in her stomach turn into a full-blown quake as she watched Khal's features turn from mild concern to disbelief before his gaze slowly rose to settle pointedly on her.

'Leave us,' he said quietly, his eyes never leaving her. It was the kind of quiet, firm voice he used when he was barely controlling his temper. The staff around him bowed their heads and left the room immediately, obeying their King's orders.

Cressida fought the urge to turn tail and run. 'What is it?' she asked, hearing the tremor in her voice.

'Why don't you read it for yourself?' He placed the file in her hands and turned his back to her, walking to the window, allowing her a moment.

Cressida scanned the file. It held an article dated that morning from an American publication, outlining very clearly a witness account to a royal scandal in the mysterious European kingdom of Monteverre. The royal scandal that had shaped her entire life.

Cressida felt a lump form in her throat as she took in the salacious headline in bold black ink.

Newly Crowned Queen of Zayyar's Illegitimate Past: the secret behind the scandalous Sandoval family revealed.

The tremor in her stomach turned to full-blown nausea as she felt her breath leave her lungs. Well, here it was, the moment she had prayed would never come to pass. Perhaps it was simply a gossip article; perhaps it was one of those rare cases where the media actually got quite close to the truth by accident but didn't actually have the evidence.

But, as she scanned through the rest of the article, she saw the name that haunted her. A name that she had found by chance at twelve years old, unknowingly setting the cogs in motion that would lead to her feeling ostracised and unwanted for evermore. She could still remember the smell of alcohol on her mother's breath the day she had told her that she was the product of an affair. Unwanted. A shameful reminder of her own mistake.

'Is this true?' Khal asked, still facing out of the window.

'Am I the shameful secret of the Sandoval royal family?' she heard her own voice say, as though from far away. 'Yes, unfortunately it's true.'

Khal turned around, reaching up to pinch the bridge of his nose. 'You did not think to disclose this information upon our marriage?'

'This information was never to be disclosed. My father… King Fabian, I mean, he and his team took extreme legal measures to ensure that it would never see the light of day.' She felt cold, her skin prickling, her insides shaking. She couldn't look at him; she couldn't see whatever expression might be in his eyes as he looked at her.

'Legal measures?'

'As far as I understand, a very large amount of money has been paid annually to this man to keep his silence on the matter.'

'Your biological father?'

Cressida nodded, the discomfort on hearing those words far too much for her to keep eye contact at all.

'You read the article?' A strange note had entered his voice. 'The last paragraph in particular?'

Cressida picked the file up from where she'd laid it on the coffee table, scanning down to the end of the article. 'Posthumous request?' she said numbly. 'He's dead?'

'The interview was released by his family, who are in control of his estate since his death, it seems.'

'It says here that he passed away four years ago.' Cressida shook her head. 'Why release this now? If they were able to break his nondisclosure upon his death.'

'Four years ago you were not the Queen of Zayyar,' Khal said with cold derision.

Cressida took a deep breath, feeling it shudder into her lungs. She closed her eyes, trying to calm the panic that was rising swiftly inside her to a raging storm. 'What are you going to do?'

Khal did not answer; instead he walked to the door and instructed his team to re-enter. The men and women filed in one by one, each one avoiding her eyes, but Cressida could feel them watching her. Judging her. All of a sudden the air was stifling in the sitting room.

'I need to go to the restroom for a moment,' she mumbled quietly, Khal barely looking her way as she slipped out of the door into the hallway beyond. Once alone, she lifted her dress up from the floor and moved quickly. She had no idea where she was going; she just had to get far away from the room full of knowing eyes that lay behind her.

CHAPTER NINE

'WHAT IS THE PLAN?' Khal addressed the head of his team. 'We have a room full of foreign dignitaries and politicians. They each have assistants and smartphones and instant updates. It's a fiasco.'

His head of PR spoke first. 'I think you need to speak on the matter as soon as possible, Your Highness. The longer it is left unaddressed, the weaker our position.'

'And what you propose I say, exactly?' Khal half laughed. 'This information comes just as much of a surprise to me as it would to them.'

'Yes, but the world cannot know that. We must act as though the Sheikha's parentage was known to you. That it was a matter of delicacy that you chose not to disclose for your wife's privacy.'

'And what is Monteverre's position on the matter?' Khal asked, feeling his fists clench at the thought of King Fabian and his underhand measures. It was likely the man did not care one ounce that his daughter had been publicly humiliated in the media. She was no longer a Sandoval, after all.

In the short time that he had been acquainted with Cressida's father, the man had shown him nothing but dishonesty and a ruthless greed that turned his stomach. King Fabian was not the kind of leader who put his people first. He was not even the kind of man to put his family first, given recent events.

And yet, when he had been contacted with the news that the youngest Princess was willing to accept the marriage, he had not hesitated to accept. Khal thought of the first night that he had met Cressida, once she had realised who he was, and he remembered her words. 'It has always been part of my duty to my kingdom...'

He had asked her numerous times if she had been forced into accepting this marriage. He had wanted to make sure that she was not entering into their union under duress...

Ignoring the sudden niggling feeling in his stomach, he looked up just as one of the junior assistants entered the room.

'The Sheikha has retired to her suite,' the young woman said.

Khal raised one brow. 'Retired? We are in the middle of a function.'

The young woman winced. 'Her Highness was quite adamant that she would not be returning, Sire. I was simply asked to convey the message.'

'I see.' Khal stood, walking towards the door before he even knew what he had planned to do. 'Keep the guests entertained. It seems I must retrieve my wife.'

Long strides and a rush of adrenaline had him at the door of Cressida's room within minutes. He did not knock, entering and closing the door with a thud behind him. She had been standing at the window but whirled around at his sudden entrance.

'I will not be abandoned in the middle of dinner.' Khal spoke evenly. It was taking all his self-control not to let his voice boom across the room with the force of his irritation. 'I understand that this situation is uncomfortable—'

'I can't go back in there.' Cressida's voice cut across him, loud and clear. 'I cannot sit and eat my dessert, knowing that the entire room is whispering about my secrets.'

The slight tremor in her voice unwound some of his irritation. She was upset; of course she would be. She had not known that her biological father was dead, that much was clear. But, apart from that, he realised that he had absolutely no idea what the rest of the story was. He had been too preoccupied with the scandal, and how to contain it. He had been Khal, Sheikh of Zayyar. While right now his wife had just needed support from her husband.

'The whole world will know within the next twenty-four hours, *habibti*.' He was surprised at the softness in his voice as he spoke. 'It is not going to go away. And it is definitely not going to get any easier just by hiding yourself away in your rooms.'

'I'm not cut out for this; I told you that before you married me. I was not given the same training to live in the limelight that my sisters were.' She inhaled deeply, turning her face away from him to look out at where the sun was setting on the horizon of the desert. 'Nothing about me is the same as my sisters, and now you know why.'

'How long have you known the truth of your parentage?'

'On some level, perhaps I always knew. Physically, I never inherited the famed Sandoval beauty. I always had the feeling that my father looked at me differently.

Almost like he held me in disdain, no matter how I be-
haved.' She moved towards the window, her long skirt
blowing slightly in the breeze that drifted in. 'When I
was twelve, I found a box hidden away in the back of my
mother's dressing room. It was filled to the brim with
letters and some photographs of a man I didn't recog-
nise. My father found me trawling through these love
letters and images. Nothing was particularly graphic or
inappropriate, of course; my mother is a queen, after
all.' A cruel laugh escaped her throat, or perhaps it
was a sob.

'What did your father do?' Khal asked.

'Oh, he never punished me, if that's what you're
thinking. He's not one for physical punishment or
outward displays of aggression.' Her eyes narrowed
slightly. 'I wonder if perhaps a good spanking might
have left less scars; I don't know. He grabbed the box, he
took me by the hand and he brought me to my mother. I
remember she was sitting drinking brandy in the salon.
She smiled at me after he made her tell me the truth. It
was the saddest smile I have ever seen.

'And then I just stood there, twelve years old, and
listened to my father spout rage and venom while my
mother stared blankly out of the window. At one point
he turned to me, photograph in his hand, and he said,
"I am not your father. He is." I will never forget that
moment as long as I live. His eyes were almost black
with rage, spittle flying out of his mouth as he spoke. I
remember flinching as he held the photograph inches
from my nose, screaming at me to look at it, to look at
him. Him being the man my mother had betrayed our
family with.'

Khal let the silence fall between them, amazed at the

lack of emotion on her pale features as she recounted such awful memories. For a moment he felt the urge to close the space between them, to reach out and take her in his arms. It was too intimate, too much emotion tangling up the logical side of his brain that he knew was the priority right now. But his wife was hurting, that much was clear. She might not show her pain, but he could see it in the way she held her shoulders pulled straight, in the way she held her chin high but her lip quivered slightly.

Making his decision, he moved to her side and took both of her hands in his own.

'When you said that you were marrying me as part of your duty,' he began, tilting her chin up so that he could see her face, 'did this secret have anything to do with it? Were you blackmailed?' He did not know what he would do if the answer was yes.

She met his eyes for a moment, the sadness he saw there so profound that he felt his breath catch.

'I was not blackmailed, Khal. My father was already planning to cancel my research work and call me back to Monteverre, whether I agreed to this marriage or not. I made the mistake of sending him a letter around the same time that Olivia had run away from your engagement offer. I told him of a job offer I had received at the university. He was furious. I might not be a Sandoval by blood but I still held the name and title. By agreeing to marry you…he said it would make him proud.' Her voice broke on the last word.

Khal felt his chest constrict, his arms surrounding her as she finally melted into him and let the tears fall. Hearing the evidence of yet more emotional manipulation by such a cruel man made the primal beast within him growl even louder. To use his daughter's love against her, to manipulate her… He took a breath, loosening his hold on her and creating enough space between them so that he could look down into her eyes.

'I will make an excuse for you; there is no reason to force you to return to the function in this kind of emotional state.'

'No.' She shook her head, standing up straight and blotting her eyes lightly with the tips of her fingers. 'It was childish of me to run off like that. Tonight is about taking my place as Sheikha. It's better if we maintain a united front, like the team said. I can hold myself together for another hour or two.'

'You are sure?' Khal frowned at the sudden change in her posture, the way she seemed to so easily switch off such deep pain and anguish.

She nodded, all the weakness from a moment before gone. Aside from a slight smudge at the corner of one eye, it would take very close scrutiny to know that she had been crying at all. She was practised in hiding her pain, he knew now. It made something inside him clench to know that she was now hiding it from him too.

The rest of the dinner passed in a blur. Cressida did not know if perhaps the news had not broken as quickly as they expected it to, or perhaps their guests were simply putting on a very convincing front. But it was a relief that no one seemed to be looking at her differently, no hushed conversations seemed to occur in her vicinity. Or perhaps her inner turmoil was such that she simply did not notice or care.

It felt as though all the energy in her body had been depleted, leaving her weak and tired. So, so tired.

The news that her biological father was dead had shocked her, even though she had never met the man. She had only ever seen his picture, and read the beautiful letters sent to her mother. Vincent was his name, a humble chauffeur. How utterly clichéd that her mother would have a sordid affair with her driver. This really was the media's dream scandal. Most likely, there would be books written. Hollywood probably had someone penning a script as they spoke.

She kept her polite smile in place as the guests began to filter out, taking the chance to slip quietly away. She had fulfilled her duty, she had sat and eaten and listened to speeches and applauded at the correct times. Now, she wanted nothing more than to collapse in her bed and bury herself beneath the covers until the rest of the world was no longer talking about her.

Khal had not spoken to her since they'd returned to the banquet; clearly he was far too preoccupied in ensuring that they retained the power in this awful situation she had created. Poor him, having shackled himself to such an unworthy bride. Heaven only knew what the Zayyari public would make of this scandal. Perhaps there would be call for an annulment of the marriage, now that it was public knowledge that her parentage was illegitimate. She was polluting the royal image of the kingdom with her scandal and secrecy.

Once in her room, she went about the ritual of allowing her maid to assist her with the more difficult garments, then dismissed the young woman for the night so that she could take her time getting ready for bed. She removed the pearl earrings from her ears, placing them delicately into the small box on her dressing table. Next, she removed the heavy necklace from her neck, taking a final moment to admire the glitter of the sapphires in the lamplight.

Standing up from her table, she took a moment to take in the designer lingerie that had been paired with her evening gown. Apparently a dress like hers required a specific cut of bra and underwear to achieve maximum effect. She had just been grateful that she wasn't forced to wear some sort of medieval corset.

The bra was definitely designed well, she smiled to herself. A movement in the mirror caught her eye, and she looked up to see Khal standing in the doorway. They both stood frozen for a moment, Cressida with one hand awkwardly cupping the lace of her bra.

'I came to talk.' He averted his eyes, seeming suddenly transfixed upon a spot on the floor. 'I'll wait in the living room.' With that, he turned around and closed the door behind him.

Cressida exhaled slowly, dropping her hand from her breast to rest at her side. A bubble of nervous laughter rose in her chest. If he didn't already think she was odd, after walking in to find her examining her own bra…

Not wanting to keep him waiting, she threw on her dressing gown, making sure it was closed tight at the front, and tied a double knot at her waist. Slipping on her silk slippers, she contemplated tying her hair into a loose bun but decided against it, considering that it had been pinned up already all evening. Most likely Khal simply wanted to give her an update on the media situation and he would be gone, leaving her free to fall into bed alone as usual.

He sat in an easy repose on her small settee, long legs casually crossed one over the other as he flipped through the fashion magazine that had been left on her coffee table.

'I just want to clarify that I don't usually stand and examine myself in the mirror like that, in case you think me awfully vain.' She kept her tone light in an effort to appear easy and unaffected by the fact that he had just witnessed her half naked. Not that that exactly mattered, considering that he had already seen her fully naked once before, but she wouldn't dwell too much on that thought if she planned to get through this conversation.

'And here I was thinking I had stumbled upon another little secret of yours.' He attempted a smile.

Cressida appreciated his attempt at humour, considering he was not usually one for jokes. She took a seat on the other side of the settee, carefully keeping the folds of her dressing gown together. For a moment she thought she saw his eyes scanning her body slowly, then he blinked and looked away.

'You disappeared tonight before I had the chance to talk further,' he said. 'I wanted to express my admiration for you this evening. Returning to that dinner could not have been easy.'

'It's easier than sitting alone with my thoughts at the moment.' Cressida shrugged.

'Why do you do that?' he asked quietly. 'I offer you a compliment and you shrug it off as though it makes you uncomfortable.'

Cressida fought the urge to squirm in her seat, feeling as though he was doing that thing where he saw right through her. He had always seen her, the real her, so much more than anyone else had. 'Okay, how about I go back in time thirty seconds and I simply say thank you?'

One corner of his mouth raised slightly, his gaze never leaving hers. 'What else would you do if you could go back in time, I wonder?'

'According to my lessons in royal interview tactics, that is the kind of question the Sheikha must never answer.'

'Never has a question been deflected with more skill.' Khal half laughed, giving her mock applause. It was strange, laughing with him after the strain of the past few hours, but at the same time it was just really nice too.

'Why did you come here?' Cressida asked. 'I mean, of course you are welcome to come here whenever you like. I just meant tonight in particular. You must have something specific you wanted to talk about.'

'I did come here to talk further about the plan for the next few days, the strategy to contain the story in the media...' He met her eyes, uncrossing his legs and sitting forward with his hands on his knees. 'My team want us to lie low for a couple of days while they assess the situation and make plans with the relevant team in Monteverre. Then we will travel over for our official visit and address the matter.'

Back to Monteverre. To confront the truth. Cressida felt anxiety rise swiftly within her but she pushed it back down.

'Are you okay? Honestly?' His eyes held hers as he reached between them to grasp her hands. 'It is all right to show me your weakness, Cressida. I won't judge you.'

Cressida felt her heart pump in her chest, hearing the gentle tone of his voice. 'I'm sorry I didn't tell you. I understand if you see me differently now. If you regret our marriage.'

His grip on her hands tightened. 'Is that what you think?'

'You seemed angry all evening. Agitated. It's an entirely valid way to feel, finding out that your wife is even less perfect than she already was.'

'I do not expect you to be perfect, Cressida. This news has come as a shock but, more than anything, I am angry for you, not towards you,' he said passionately. 'And as for regretting our marriage...' He shook his head.

She inhaled deeply, hardly believing, as a rueful smile crossed his lips.

'Some of my agitation likely stems from how utterly beautiful you look tonight and how frustrated I am at not being able to touch you. I haven't been able to take my eyes off you all evening,' he said evenly, his gaze locked on hers. 'It has been a week since I had you in my arms and I still remember every single moment with painful clarity.'

Cressida took a deep breath, the intensity of his gaze on hers making her heart skitter uncomfortably in her chest. She felt restless and yet glued to the spot all at once.

'We said that we would stick with the original plan. But I think that my plan changed the moment I danced with you in the club in London.' His voice seemed lower all of a sudden...huskier. 'I held on to my plan because that's simply what I do. I keep things under control. But it seems that my control does not exist when it comes to you, Cressida.'

'What are you saying?' she asked nervously, not exactly sure what she wanted to hear. She wanted him to want her, but not just as a sexual distraction until they wore each other out or got sick of each other.

'I'm saying that the tidy little red line that I drew around both of our separate circles has been blurred and broken to a point where they seem to be melding into one, whether we will them to or not. So now it seems we face a choice. We can choose to completely separate our lives in such a way that we are very rarely in each other's presence at all. Or we can ignore the red lines completely and see what happens.'

'A world without red lines…' Cressida said slowly, seeing the tension in his body as he awaited her response. 'It seems very uncertain for a man who loves certainty.'

'The only thing that I'm certain about at the moment is that if I don't have you in my arms in the next five seconds I may very well burst out of my skin or erupt into flames where I sit.'

Cressida smiled, a shiver of anticipation running down her spine. 'Oh, don't do that. I've grown quite attached to this sofa,' she said, her voice taking on a sultry tone that shocked her.

A slow smile spread across Khal's lips, 'Well, it seems your choice has been made.' He closed the distance between them in record time, his body covering hers at the same moment his lips moulded against her own.

CHAPTER TEN

THE KISS WAS filled with every ounce of tension and frustration that she had felt herself. She had dreamt of his kisses, had tried her hardest to remember what it felt like to have his lips on hers in case she never felt it again. And yet now that his lips were on hers once more she wondered how she had ever forgotten the feeling. It was so familiar now, like coming home. Dangerously comfortable and yet feverishly exciting all at once.

Cressida felt as though her heart might beat completely out of her chest. What was it about kissing this man that sent every single hormonal impulse in her body into chaos? And not only that, she wanted to say things to him. Do things that made her shocked. She reached out to run her fingers down the bared skin of his chest, spreading his shirt collar wide so that she could touch him just as he had touched her.

Khal's hands encircled her wrists, moving her backwards until she lay back on the sofa, her nightgown spread wide to expose her partially clothed body. He pressed his mouth to the skin above her navel, moving inch by tantalising inch lower, all the while maintaining eye contact. The heat between her legs heightened to a blazing fire and she could not help but reach her fingers towards him, not sure if she wanted to stop him or tell him to move faster to his destination.

'What do you want me to do, Cressida…?' He spoke each syllable with a caress of his lips against her sensitive skin, his large muscular hands gripping her hips.

She breathed hard, hardly able to control the small movements her pelvis made as his lips reached the edge of her lace underwear. 'I want your mouth to touch me… there.' No longer able to be embarrassed by her own words, she moaned as he drew his fingers up along the thin material.

'Right here?' he asked, repeating the movement and groaning as she arched herself against his touch. He stopped speaking then, pulling her underwear down over her hips and throwing them over his shoulder.

The first touch of his tongue along her bared flesh was like nothing she could have ever expected. It was as though her entire body lit up from the inside, warmth spinning upwards along her nerve endings like fireworks. The second touch was even more intense as he drew his tongue slowly along the very centre of her, knowing exactly where would give her the most pleasure. She arched her hips, needing to move against him rather than lying flat and limp. She could not have stayed still if she'd tried, especially once he moved into a smooth rhythm. She had thought the first part was amazing, but it seemed he had more tricks up his sleeve. After a moment, he shifted, looking up at her while he slid his index finger down and slowly into her tight heat. Cressida tilted her head back as he resumed his tongue mastery now with the addition of moving his finger against a spot inside her that she had not known existed. When he added a second finger she thought she might combust on the spot, the feeling of fullness was so intense. Her heart began to pound and she was sure the tension could build no further, the slow tremendous build up like nothing she had ever felt before.

When she finally shattered, she thought she gripped his hair so tightly she was sure it must have been painful. But she was much too busy being overcome by wave after wave of devastating pleasure to care too much. Eyes closed, she was vaguely aware of Khal moving up over her, his mouth laying kisses along her neck.

'You are even more beautiful when you climax.'

She smiled, unable to feel embarrassed after the earth-shattering bliss of what she had just experienced. She felt beautiful when he looked at her this way, as though he could devour her in a single bite.

She reached to his waistband and unzipped the front of his trousers quickly before she lost her nerve. She wanted all of him. It seemed unfair that she was completely nude while he was still dressed. As though reading her thoughts, Khal pulled his shirt over his head and helped her by pulling the trousers off the rest of the way.

She began her exploration on his bare chest, feeling the strength of his pectorals under her fingertips and moving lower to where his abdomen dipped in at the hips. It was the body of a leader, a warrior. Her protector, she thought with a quiet ferocity. She wanted to show him the same care and pleasure that he had shown her, but fear of her own lack of practice made her settle for encircling his length with her hand instead. He thrust forward into her palm, a low hiss escaping his teeth as he exhaled hard. She stroked him, slowly at first then increasing her pace.

'I need to be inside you,' he growled low in his

throat, pulling her hands above her head and moving over her to crush her mouth against his.

She luxuriated in the feeling of all that powerful bare muscle pressed flush against every inch of her. She could feel the heavy heat of his arousal pressing against the top of her thigh and she rocked against him, showing him with her body that she had never wanted anything more in her life.

Khal willed himself to take it slow when all he wanted to do was plunge hard and fast into the delicious heat he knew awaited him. She moved against him again, sliding her slippery heat against him. She was trying to kill him.

He placed one hand on her hip, stilling her as he entered. Her body grasped him so tightly he seriously doubted his ability to last longer than ten seconds.

He wondered if anything on earth was as perfect as the sheer pleasure of being buried fully inside her molten heat. Her body gripped him like a vice, such an absolutely perfect fit it took every ounce of the patience and skill he had to hold himself still and allow her a moment to adjust. The torment of waiting heightened every nerve ending in his body, so much so that he could feel his climax building almost immediately. He leaned down, taking one hard nipple in his mouth and grazing his teeth along the pink flesh. She gasped, her muscles relaxing and tensing as she took him deeper, squeezing him tight.

'You drive me to madness, *habibti*,' he gritted, burying his face in the hollow of her neck as he moved slowly against her. Taking his time to let her catch up, urging her body upwards to join him. He felt her pulse quicken under his lips, her skin salty with the barest sheen of sweat. She was lost to it just as he was, the storm of sensation dancing and growing in the delicious friction of their bodies.

He groaned as his climax approached, moving harder against her and reaching down to caress the sensitive spot he knew would tip her over the edge. He knew the very moment she began to fall, her eyes meeting his for a split second with nothing but raw, primal need in their depths. That was all it took—one look and he could hold out no longer.

Mine, the demon inside him growled. With a hoarse cry he gave in to the pleasure and fully lost himself in Cressida's heat.

There was a man in her bed. Cressida smiled to herself, taking in Khal's glorious muscular form spread out alongside her. Her body felt stiff in places she hadn't known she could strain but nothing could ruin this for her. They had made love once more last night after Khal had carried her to the bathroom and showed her the hidden pleasures that could be found in the shower.

Sex was so much more than she had ever imagined it to be. It had felt like a meeting of their bodies, like two parts joining together in a mutual dance. And what a dance it was with Khal…

She remembered his words the first time he had taken her into his arms on that nightclub dancefloor, about dance being a temptation. The thought made her smile quietly to herself.

He stirred alongside her and she closed her eyes, not quite brave enough to admit she had been awake and ogling him while he slept. A hand splayed across her stomach, sliding across her skin for a moment before she felt his lips touch the delicate skin of her breast.

'Keep your eyes closed,' he murmured. 'We can pretend that you are still asleep and haven't ruined my very specific plans to wake you.'

Cressida shivered, opening her eyes just as he moved over her, kissing a path down the valley of her breasts and over her stomach. His lips were like hot silk moving over her skin, familiar and tantalising. He paid special attention to each hip before deftly bypassing the place she ached for him most in favour of laying a trail of kisses down the insides of each thigh.

'That's not fair.' She tried to laugh but the sound came out a breathy moan. She hadn't even known she was capable of making such feminine sounds until Khal.

'Never let it be said that the great Sheikh is not a fair man,' he teased, moving down to settle between her thighs with dark promise. She did not tense at all as one finger slowly entered her, closely followed by a second. She gasped, feeling him hit just the right spot and begin to work it in a perfect rhythm. Her hips bucked upwards, the pleasure so acute it was almost painful. Spreading her wide, his tongue darted over her sex once, twice…three times, but not quite allowing her to move towards climax.

Cressida sighed, looking up at him just as he moved over her. She pressed her hands on his chest, rising up from the bed so that they both kneeled facing each other. She looked down at his impressive length, running one fingertip along the silky-smooth skin before encircling him with her hand and meeting his eyes purposefully.

'I want to return the favour,' she said boldly.

Khal raised one brow, lying back on the bed in silent invitation. He was not submissive in bed. He was controlled and knew exactly what to do to drive them both over the edge. She wanted the chance to learn how to drive him crazy, just like he did to her. She leaned over him, taking him into her mouth with one smooth movement. He tasted like sex, the action so utterly erotic she felt herself grind her hips a little. One strong hand moved to slide up the outside of her thigh, dropping a light smack on the curve of her behind. He repeated the action and she bit her lip, amazed that she enjoyed it.

'That's it. Just like that.' He exhaled hard.

Typical Khal, she thought, still trying to maintain control. Not this time. She took him deeper into her mouth, feeling his taut stomach muscles shudder beneath her hands.

'I could have you do this all day,' he growled, letting his hand coil into the length of her hair, stopping her movement but still not withdrawing entirely. 'But I cannot wait another moment before I can be inside you again.'

She sat back, running her fingers down his powerful thighs and trying to take a mental photograph of this moment. She did not know how long this mindless passion between them would last. But right now it felt as though they were the only two people in the world and she wanted to savour every moment. His hand encircled her wrist, gently tugging her so that she lay draped over him. She kissed him, softly at first before letting her arousal take over and taking the kiss deeper. Her mind no longer intruded, her body recognising his and knowing just what lay in store.

Strong hands gripped her hips. He thrust upwards, and both of them filled the room with the kind of throaty moan that only came with that very first joining. He thrust deep, filling her to the hilt, and withdrew halfway before he let his hands drift to his sides and went still.

'Show me how you like it,' he said, lying back to watch her with a look of deep male appreciation.

She bit her lip, feeling momentarily vulnerable with his eyes devouring her, but the delicious slide of him inside her was enough to move her thoughts elsewhere quickly enough. She moved over him slowly, finding her rhythm and gasping at the sensation of being filled so very deeply.

She trusted him completely, she realised, suddenly unable to look at him as the force of her emotions began to build, along with her climax. He moved, sitting up so that their chests were only inches apart; his hands on her hips kept her rhythm in check as he thrust in time with her. After the mind-exploding pleasure of their orgasms had passed there was only silence, and then the sound of their laboured breathing. Khal moved away first, darting a quick glance in her direction before lying flat on his back.

Something in his eyes told her that he felt it too, this painful closeness. She inhaled, feeling a lingering tightness in her chest from the force of keeping her emotions in check. She stood from the bed, moving to the bathroom on shaky legs and closing the door gently behind her.

This was so much more than feeling overwhelmed by sex, she thought, biting her lip at her own naiveté. She had known she was in danger from the moment he had looked into her eyes in that wedding tent. He had started out as the man she had been forced to choose and somehow wound up being her perfect fit. Her lover. The word seemed to caress something deep inside her, a tiny speck of romanticism that she would never have dreamed existed within her cynical heart. But there it was, clear as day. And, just as that speck began to glow and blossom, realisation dawned that she had done what she had vowed not to do.

She had let her emotions get involved. She had fallen in love with her husband.

Khal woke with a start, a light sheen of sweat on his chest as he sat up in the unfamiliar bedroom. It took a moment to realise where he was. He stood up, walking to the long terrace doors and opening them a few inches to take in a breath of fresh air. The city of Valar spread out before him in a glittering blanket of lights. The dream had been much the same as it always was. Priya's voice haunting him, reminding him of his unworthiness, only tonight she had not been alone. Beside her, Cressida had appeared, tears falling from her eyes.

He contemplated slipping out to his own room, but immediately disregarded the idea as cowardly. He was not some kind of lothario who slipped in and out of bedrooms in the darkness. He splashed some cold water on his face and went back into the bedroom. The light beside the bed was on and to his dismay he found Cressida was sitting up, waiting for him.

'I had not meant to wake you.' Khal lay heavily back down onto the bed, turning on his side to take in the beautiful sight that greeted him. Cressida lay back against the pillows, ash-blonde hair spilling around her bare shoulders and the satin sheets tucked demurely under her arms to cover her chest. The innocent display of modesty was a delicious distraction from his troubled thoughts; he could think of no better way to redirect his mind than by peeling away those sheets, inch by glorious inch...

'You were talking in your sleep...' Cressida disturbed his train of thought, a nervous tone to her quiet voice '... I was debating whether or not to wake you but then I heard you get up... I wasn't sure if perhaps you were sleepwalking.'

'I hope I at least said something entertaining,' he joked easily, but still he wondered how much she might have gleaned from his night-time ramblings.

Cressida did not smile. 'I believe that you...you were dreaming of your wife.'

He could hear the sadness in her voice, the uncertainty. 'You are my wife. Let us not get mixed up on that fact, *habibti.*'

'You were saying her name.' She took her lip between her teeth, worrying it slightly, weighing up her words before she spoke. 'Priya. Do you dream of her often?'

Khal exhaled, deeply uncomfortable with the turn this conversation had taken. He had never spoken to a soul about the dreams that'd plagued him since Priya's death. How their final conversation seemed to haunt him so heavily. And even now, four years later, the dreams would come back every now and then. It tended to happen at very inopportune times, like when he slept in a jet surrounded by staff or the first night that he slept beside his new wife after making love... He silently cursed himself.

'I'm not exactly sure what triggers the dream, maybe

stress or lack of sleep. It just kind of happens every once in a while.' He curled one arm behind his head and studied the ceiling for a moment, knowing the conversation had only begun, judging by the curious look on Cressida's face.

'No one ever seems to talk of how she died,' Cressida said slowly. 'It's as though it's some great big secret. Ironic, coming from me, I know.'

Khal attempted a smile but found the muscles in his face seemed suddenly tight. He did not speak of Priya's death to anyone. He never had. Other than to aid in the investigations into her accident, no one addressed the subject and he certainly did not bring it into conversation. It felt as though every comfortable boundary in his life had begun to slowly erode from the moment he had met Cressida.

'You don't have to speak about it,' she said quickly, feigning a sudden interest in the pattern on the sheets that covered her abdomen. 'It's probably quite presumptuous of me to even ask. I'm sorry.'

Khal felt like an utter ass, seeing the look on her face. Of course she had the right to ask; they were married and he had just been speaking another woman's name in their bed. The rules surrounding their marriage were still blurred at present, neither of them knowing exactly what was okay or not. The initial agreement for a marriage in name only had most definitely been broken, but it left them in a kind of limbo. They were not man and wife in the truest sense, but neither were they the kind of formal arrangement he had originally envisioned. He knew that right now was most definitely one of those moments where he needed to do the difficult thing.

'It's not something I'm usually comfortable talking

about,' he said slowly, watching as her eyes raised up to meet his. He reached out and laid his hand over hers on the sheets. 'But you spoke through your own discomfort; therefore perhaps it is only fair that I do the same.'

'You don't have to…' Cressida began quickly.

'I want to,' he said, surprised to realise that he was speaking the truth. 'I told you once before that my marriage was not all that it seemed. To the public we were untouchable. I was the picture-perfect husband and she the perfect wife.' He shook his head, a cruel laugh escaping from his lips. 'Not a single soul knows the last words she ever spoke to me… The words that haunt my dreams at night. She told me that she would rather die than be my wife a moment longer.' Khal turned his head, expecting to see disgust in Cressida's eyes. But what he saw there instead was more uncomfortable. Pity. Oh, how he had despised that look of pity on people's faces in the months following his wife's death.

'Couples have arguments all of the time,' Cressida began.

'It was not the first time that she had spoken in that way.' Khal shook his head. 'I was not the best husband, by any standard.' She didn't understand; she didn't realise that when Priya had said those words she had truly meant them.

'How awful, to have that memory in your mind,' Cressida said softly, covering his hand with hers.

Khal inhaled deeply, wanting to recoil from the pity he could hear in her voice. 'You wanted to know how she died. I'll tell you, but you must forgive me if I still hold some anger.' He had unconsciously begun to tap his foot at some point, a nervous gesture that he constantly tried to overcome since teenage years. Kings did not fidget, he remembered his father telling him. Control—it was always about showing control.

'There has never been a definitive answer on how she came to be on the road that she was, at the time that she was. One point of view is that she was on her way to meet her lover. I was aware that she had been unfaithful to me on a number of occasions in the later years of our marriage.' Khal saw a look of shock cross Cressida's features, followed by a brief hint of anger. 'Another view is that she purposely drove her car over the side of the ravine at a high speed in order to end her own life.'

Cressida winced, her grip tightening on his hand.

'In Zayyari culture, both of those possibilities spell out shame. I was not prepared to have her name sullied, so the nature of her death was never disclosed. The perceived secrecy led to speculation and rumours. Most of which involved various theories of how I was a ruthless barbarian who had arranged his wife's murder. Or worse, that I had killed her myself and had the truth covered up.

'I was assured that her death was instantaneous. For that I was grateful.' He closed his eyes for a moment, trying to ignore the onslaught of memories. The smell of burning rubber in the air as he had moved down the side of the sandbank, his guards shouting at him to stop. He remembered watching as one of his sports cars was hoisted from the shallow water. Priya's lifeless body had already been transported to the morgue where he had identified her, but for some reason Khal had needed to see the car. He had needed to see the place where it had happened, to make sense of it all.

'Nothing about it made sense; that was the worst part

to accept. The investigators told me that there was no way to prove if the car had been tampered with, considering it had to be destroyed upon transportation to be impounded.' He shook his head, sitting up straight. 'The idea that her anger at me led to her driving dangerously never sat well with me. I have spent years trying to find evidence that someone deliberately caused the accident other than Priya herself. It's only now…saying it out loud… that I realise maybe that's just my way of coping with my own guilt and sense of powerlessness.'

Cressida leaned forward, pressing her cheek against his bare back and sliding her arm around his abdomen. The gesture was so intimate and so comforting that for a moment he felt himself tightening, the urge to pull away strong. But then the warmth of her skin seeped into his own and he found himself accepting her comfort, grateful for the fact that for once he was not alone in his recollection of these painful memories.

They sat in silence for a while, Cressida listening to the beat of his heart thumping in rhythm with her own. 'I find it hard to believe that you were ever a bad husband.'

To her surprise she felt him tense beneath her skin, pulling away from her slightly. She sat back, wondering if perhaps she had touched a nerve even after all he had just disclosed.

'We had a son,' Khal said, a strange emptiness to his voice as he spoke. 'He never lived, stillborn in the eighth month of pregnancy. But we had a son.'

Cressida felt something inside her break as the words hit her with full force. She had no idea what it was like to bear that kind of tragedy and pain in one's life. The very idea of Khal going through such a loss was unbearable.

'When I say that I was a bad husband, I don't mean that I was a bit selfish or that I forgot to put the toilet seat down. I was a bad husband because my wife's needs were never taken into consideration. All that mattered was ensuring that my need for tight security and safety was prioritised. I overreacted to everything. She got swarmed in the markets once, early on in her pregnancy, and I decided that I needed to keep her under tighter security, even if it meant keeping her confined to the palace. Priya told me on numerous occasions that she was unhappy but the final straw was when she was rushed to hospital, pregnant and terrified. I was halfway across the world being the grand Sheikh of Zayyar. And when I was finally given the news a day later, there was absolutely nothing I could do. We had only been married a year at that point.'

'You blame yourself for so much…' Cressida began, not quite knowing what to say in the face of such an admission.

'I'm sorry. I said that I don't like to share and yet here I am, unable to stop.' He turned, taking her hands in his and looking deep into her eyes.

'There is no need to explain yourself to me,' Cressida said firmly. 'I am simply grateful that you trusted me enough to share what you have.'

He nodded once, taking her in his arms. The embrace began innocently enough, but then the sheet slipped down between them and suddenly she was being swept away on another wave of passion. Their lovemaking this time was slower, a tentative sliver of intimacy seeming to show in the way he held her face in his hands as he kissed her and looked deep into her eyes. Afterwards, he fell into a deep sleep with impressive speed, leaving Cressida staring up at the ceiling, physically satisfied but emotionally distracted.

She found herself absolutely livid that he had been subjected to such harsh scrutiny in his time of grief.

The world lauded her own father, a man who had held his wife and daughters to emotional ransom their whole lives, and yet Khal was shunned, based on rumours and gossip. She felt something within her changing, a strange protectiveness of this new life she had entered into. It scared her, to think that she felt such loyalty to a man she had only known a matter of weeks now. But she did trust him with all of her heart. It was keeping that heart protected when it was becoming more and more in danger of being broken...that was the real problem.

CHAPTER ELEVEN

AFTER THREE FULL days of an impromptu honeymoon spent mostly in bed, Cressida mourned the arrival of their departure for the official visit to Monteverre. They spent a large portion of the flight hidden away in the master bedroom. While Khal might have introduced her to the pleasures of the mile-high club, she had the pleasure of giving him a tour of her home town through her own eyes once they touched down.

Her decision to leave Monteverre at the age of nineteen to study abroad had held no bearing on her love for her kingdom. She had simply needed freedom from the oppressive disdain of her parents and the effort of hiding her secret from her siblings.

Even as their limousine moved slowly around the main square and she pointed out her favourite ice cream shop and the library where she had spent many an afternoon hiding away, she felt anxiety rising steadily within her. The thought of speaking to her sisters now that they had been made aware of the great family secret was daunting. At least, with her parents, she knew what to expect. She didn't know if Olivia and Eleanor would be upset, hurt or even angry at her for keeping such a secret.

Truthfully, she did not know if Olivia would show up at all. Last she had heard, she and her fiancé Roman were sailing around the Caribbean after becoming formally engaged shortly before Cressida had moved to Zayyar.

'You are very quiet, *habibti*,' Khal said as they shared a speciality Monteverrian vanilla ice cream on a narrow side street. 'Don't think I haven't noticed that you are delaying our arrival at the palace.'

Cressida bit her lower lip, hating that he seen through her so easily but also enjoying the fact just a little. 'I'm delaying the unknown. My sisters were always kept in the dark when it came to the secret of my parentage. As far as they knew, there was nothing different about me other than the obvious facts that I have poor fashion sense and a strange attachment to books.'

'I disagree, your fashion sense is no longer poor since you met me.' He jabbed, smiling as she reached out to smudge ice cream on his nose in retaliation. 'Your sisters may be a bit hurt at being kept in the dark, but they will not love you any less.'

'I hope you are right.' Cressida sighed.

They finished their ice creams and finally there was nothing else to do but make their grand arrival at the palace. Usually a high-profile guest was welcomed in grand style, with all the staff lined up at the foot of the wide concrete steps while the Royal family stood waiting at the top. Today, the steps were empty save for a single butler, who stood at the end. Cressida recognised him as Hansel, the second most senior member of the royal house staff. A harsh laugh escaped her throat at the thought that her father had not even deemed her arrival home after almost five years away to be worthy of the head butler.

'Your Highnesses, allow me to be the first to congratulate you on your recent nuptials and to formally welcome you back to Monteverre.' The older man bowed, escorting them inside and down the long familiar corridors to the grand salon.

Inside, the Sandoval family waited, her mother and sister sitting down while her father stood poised at the mantelpiece, just as she'd expected. It was his usual show of force, he was a tall man and he liked to stand in the position of power in a room when welcoming guests.

She had almost forgotten that Khal was by her side until her father stepped forward, greeting him before he greeted his own daughter.

'Welcome back to my humble kingdom, Sheikh Khalil,' King Fabian said loudly. 'I believe you have already been introduced to my eldest daughter, Crown Princess Eleanor.'

Khal glanced uncomfortably from Cressida to her father, before stepping forward and making his introduction to her older sister.

Eleanor was thinner than she remembered; that was the first thought Cressida had before her sister stepped forward suddenly and embraced her.

'Cress, it has been far too long.' Eleanor did not gush; there was nothing false about the way she held the embrace for a long moment before pulling away. For a moment it almost felt as though they were children again, before anything had ever changed.

The moment did not last long, however, her father booming across the little interlude in his usual fashion.

'And here she is, the woman of the hour,' he pronounced with mock pride.

Cressida felt Khal stiffen beside her, his hand tightening on hers.

'Father, I hope you are well.' She opted for the polite approach, ignoring the urge to simply speak her mind and address the very large elephant present in the room.

'I'm quite well, considering the stress that I and the royal team have been under for the past three days.' His lips tightened in what she supposed was an attempt at a smile. 'I doubt you've been put under much pressure, hiding out there in the desert.'

He looked to Khal in a very male attempt at camaraderie, clearly expecting her husband to share in his joke. Khal did not.

'Perhaps we should take things to a more business setting. Leave the women to catch up. It has been such a long time since Cressida has seen her family.'

Cressida tried not to react to the way the King referred to her mother and sister as her family, not his. He had no need to hide his true feelings now, she supposed. She had never been a Sandoval by birth but now she was no longer even a Sandoval by name. He could pretend that she had never existed and never feel the difference.

'This matter concerns your daughter just as much as it concerns our kingdoms—' Khal began, his shoulders straightening.

'No, you should go. You are much better at all of this.' Cressida squeezed her husband's hand lightly. 'I trust you to speak on my behalf.'

'You are sure?' He dipped his head, speaking quietly near her ear.

Cressida nodded, smiling as he placed a delicate kiss

on her palm and left the room with a few long powerful strides, her father at his heels.

'So you found love, after all.' Her mother's voice drifted across the room.

Cressida had almost forgotten that her mother was there at all, considering she had not stood once since she had entered the room. 'We have a comfortable arrangement. It's more than I could have hoped for, considering the circumstances.' Cressida spoke evenly.

'What your father and I had... Sorry, King Fabian and I...' Her mother cleared her throat suddenly, the first sign of emotion crossing heavily lined features. 'Our arranged marriage was comfortable at best. Dangerously passionate at worst.' She took a long sip of her brandy, rising to her feet and swaying slightly. 'What you want is something in the middle, something warm that will last, not burn itself out before you've even had a chance.'

Eleanor cleared her throat, ever the peacemaker of the family. 'He seems quite fond of you,' she offered kindly. 'I'm happy for you, little sister.'

'I was nervous about coming here today, considering what has been said.' She met her older sister's eyes, feeling her voice quivering slightly. 'You must know that I would have told you, had I been allowed to.'

'Yes, yes.' Queen Aurelia sighed heavily, making her way slowly across the room towards the sideboard and the brandy decanter that stood upon it. 'We would all have done a great many things, had we been allowed to.'

Something within Cressida seemed to stretch thin and snap apart. Years of hurt and emotional pain rose to the surface, her temper rising with it.

'Your attitude is appalling, Mother.' Eleanor spoke

first, surprising Cressida with the backbone in her voice. Her elder sister had always been the strong, silent one. Never sharing the details of her own seemingly perfect marriage. Always simply moving forward with her duty and not getting involved in any of the family politics that might have arisen.

'My attitude?' Queen Aurelia laughed, filling up her glass almost to the top with amber liquid, not seeming to care that it was barely midday. 'At least I did not run away the first chance I got. At least I put my family first.'

'Is that how you justify your actions to yourself?' Cressida asked quietly. 'I have often wondered if you were entirely oblivious or if you simply never cared about your children or the consequences that your selfishness had on them.'

'Selfishness?' Her mother's eyes widened, her hand abandoning the brandy glass entirely as she swung around to face her two daughters across the grand salon. 'I gave up everything for my children. Don't you dare speak of things when you have no idea of the truth.'

'What have you ever given up?' Cressida shook her head, amazed at the vitriol and the energy in her mother's voice all of a sudden. The woman had been a living ghost for as long as she could remember, now all of a sudden she seemed full of life as she defended her own poor choices.

Queen Aurelia shook her head, emotion seeming to overtake her momentarily as she turned her back to them and walked towards the window. Her pale blonde hair caught the rays of sunlight as she stood silently for a moment and looked out at the sea in the distance.

'Did you know that he had died?' Queen Aurelia

finally asked, turning slightly to meet Cressida's eyes for the first time.

Cressida did not need to ask who she was speaking of; the emotion in her mother's eyes spoke clearly enough. By her side she could see Eleanor begin twisting her hands together, a rare show of discomfort from the Crown Princess.

'I think perhaps I will go and sit in on the meeting,' Eleanor said quickly. 'Perhaps you would both like a moment alone.'

Before Cressida had a moment to respond, Eleanor swept from the room. Her mother turned fully to look at her, still waiting for her answer.

'No, I did not know. The newspaper article was the first I had heard of it.'

Silence fell once again in the room, the only sound a gentle sniff as her mother took out a handkerchief and gently dabbed her eyes. 'I did not have lovers, despite whatever poison Fabian may have put in your mind. I had one true love and I never had the chance to say goodbye to him.'

Tears streamed down her mother's face in earnest now, though she tried to turn away.

Cressida took a handkerchief from her purse, walking to her mother's side and offering it.

'You hated me for it. I saw it on your face the day that he dragged you into my room with my letters in his hand.' Pain was evident in her mother's tight features as she reached out to take Cressida's hand in her own. 'I have never been good at communicating with my children. I have never been good at communicating at all. I have wasted so much time.'

Cressida could hardly believe what she was hearing.

This was all she had ever wanted as a child . For her mother to sit her down and explain it to her. To show her that she wasn't the awful mistake that her father saw her as. Even if one of her parents truly loved and accepted her, it would have been enough. It would have made her feel less alone. But seeing her mother now, so broken and lonely, she did not say any of that. Instead she simply embraced her and held her while racking sobs filled the air around them.

'I loved Vincent with all of my heart, you see. He was the only one who listened to me, who made me feel protected. I never told him that he was going to become a father. I think, had he known, he never would have allowed me to stay here. I thought that I was doing what was best for you and your sisters… I thought that I could fix things with Fabian. But he never forgave me, despite me knowing that he'd been taking mistresses for years. He had left me feeling unwanted and abandoned in our marriage long before I strayed. But my mistake carried a lasting consequence, one that he could use against me and hold me to ransom with, and so I drank to avoid the misery. I slowly retreated from my life.

'When you found out the truth, I tried to contact Vincent, fearing what your father might do. I found out that he had married. He was happy, so I stayed away. I dreamed of him coming back for me, fool in love that I was. But I had broken his heart when I refused to go with him before, and so he took the money your father offered and we never heard from him again.'

Cressida fought the lump of emotion in her chest at the pain that spilled from her mother after decades of withheld emotion.

'You could have talked to me,' she said quietly. 'If

anyone in this family would understand feeling alone and unwanted it is me.'

'Cressida... I stayed in Monteverre to give you a better life and it seems as though I achieved the exact opposite. I was selfish. I let my own pain distract me from being there as a mother. You look so much like your father... Every time I looked at you for the first few years I cried. The weight of it was too much for me so I ran from it. I was a coward. I still am, really.'

'You don't have to be,' Cressida said simply. 'Your children are adults now.'

Queen Aurelia shook her head slowly. 'I have no-where else to be. Not any longer.' She stared out of the window for a moment before turning back. 'I just needed you to understand... I could never regret the choice that resulted in the happiest time in my life, de-spite the fact that I knew it was wrong in so many ways. That love resulted in you, Cressida.'

They were interrupted by staff coming to ask the Queen for instructions for that evening's dinner. Cressida took the opportunity to slip away under the guise of retrieving her older sister so that she might have a moment to breathe and gather her own thoughts in the aftermath of such a tumultuous conversation.

As she wandered through the halls of her childhood home in search of Eleanor, she found her mind lingering on the first words her mother had spoken to her. *'So you found love after all,'* she had said. Knowing now what her mother had been through in her own pursuit of love, the statement stuck in her mind. She desperately wanted to go back and ask what she had meant. Had she seen something in Khal's face? A gesture perhaps, or the way his eyes lingered on her? Did she know how to tell if a man was falling in love, even if he had sworn against it?

There really was no point in pretending any longer that she was any different to her mother when it came to seeking acceptance and love. And it seemed she had just the same knack for getting herself into trouble.

She had fallen madly, deeply, irrevocably in love with a man who would never feel the same.

'I see no further point in avoiding the reason why we are here. You invited us here to discuss strategy, did you not?' Khal spoke coolly from where he sat in King Fabian's large study. The man had been blathering on in detail about the extremely positive financial reports that had just been published in the Monteverrian parliament. Khal did not have time to soothe the King's fragile ego at present and found his patience had worn utterly thin since entering into his presence.

'We are still awaiting members of your team, I believe,' one of King Fabian's chief aides said in his monotone voice.

'My team will jump in when they arrive.' Khal opened the large black file that his personal secretary handed him. 'I will begin with a report on what Zayyar has done since we received first notification of this breach. Since this story broke my team and I have received minor retractions from three of the major global news sources. We have released intimate photographs of our wedding in order to redirect media attention and we have also initiated investigations into the nature of Queen Cressida's rights with regard to the legal agreements that were signed twelve years ago.'

'Have you indeed?' King Fabian's eyes narrowed.

'I'm glad that you are assuming responsibility for your *Queen*. I had half expected you to try to shirk off the duty to me.'

Khal flattened his palms on the table, inhaling deeply against his sudden urge to resort to physical violence. 'As this matter preceded our union, Cressida was insistent that your government have their say in the PR, considering that it is the Sandoval name being dragged through the mud. Believe me, had the decision been solely mine, I would not have been so merciful.'

'Merciful?' King Fabian's eyes bulged. 'You seem to have developed quite a *tendre* for your convenient bride, considering she was a poor replacement for the one you truly wanted. How is Roman Lazarov these days?'

Khal smiled at the obvious barb. 'If this is how you conduct political meetings, I can see how you brought your kingdom to such a spectacular ruin in such a short time.'

Both men stood up from the table just as the door burst open and the remainder of Khal's team entered.

'Apologies for the delay, Your Highness,' said the chief of his foreign affairs team, out of breath. 'There has been an urgent development from Zayyar.'

'Well, spit it out. We've been waiting long enough,' King Fabian said impatiently.

Khal nodded once to the man. 'If it is urgent and it involves Monteverre, go ahead.'

The man looked momentarily unsure of himself, adjusting his collar as though it was too tight around his neck. 'It seems…that the marriage agreement between Monteverre and Zayyar has been called into question,' he said slowly, drawing a sheaf of documents from his briefcase.

'That agreement has been signed and done with,' Fabian exclaimed, the rims of his eyes turning an angry red. 'Whatever underhand treachery this is, I won't tolerate it for one moment. Not one!'

'Called into question, how, exactly?' Khal ignored the other man's outburst, feeling a strange floating sensation in his solar plexus.

'Well, Your Highness, Zayyari law demands clear and truthful reporting of parentage. Both biological and legal. Parliament has proposed to nullify the marriage on the grounds that your bride forged her documentation.'

CHAPTER TWELVE

'NULLIFY,' KHAL REPEATED, the word tasting sour on his tongue. 'Even if the marriage has been consummated?'

'If you rule in its favour, yes. You hold the deciding vote, Sire.'

'I called this meeting in order to reach an agreement to manage a scandal, not create an entirely new one,' King Fabian's voice growled from the other side of the table.

'Do you deny that you deliberately withheld vital information in order to expedite my marriage to your daughter?' Khal met the King's eyes.

'I am her father by law,' Fabian said rather weakly.

'Funny how you find that so easy to say now that you see your upward financial swing could be at risk.'

'Are you going to do as they say, then?'

Khal could see the barest hint of fear in the slight widening of the other man's eyes. He momentarily contemplated launching into a list of reasons why he would not be discussing his plans with the man who had emotionally blackmailed his own daughter into marrying a stranger, but he found he had suddenly lost all desire to waste his energy a moment longer. He instructed his team to close the meeting on his behalf and quickly excused himself from the room. He knew he should go to Cressida immediately and tell her everything that had been said. But what exactly would he say?

His thoughts took him out into the grounds of the palace, memory directing him to where he knew a small collection of stallions were kept in a paddock. He had spent some time in Monteverre while negotiating the beginning of the marriage deal that would change his life so completely. He chose a large Arabian named Bruno and borrowed a pair of boots from the groomsman. The paddock was not as long as his desert outlands in Zayyar but it served its purpose, giving both him and the horse just enough space in which to race out their excess energy and quiet their minds.

He thought of Cressida's face when she'd spoken of her work, of the life she'd lived in London before he'd come crashing into it. She had told him she felt truly happy in that old life. Would she ever truly feel at peace as Sheikha of Zayyar? She had said time and time again that she was not suited to a public role. That she missed the solitude of her library and the simplicity of a private existence.

Could he really deny her the chance to turn back the hands of time and make a choice based solely on what she wanted to do? These thoughts haunted him even after the sun began to dip low in the sky. Realising he had spent longer than intended out of the palace, he released the stallion to the groomsman and made his way back inside.

They had been assigned a guest suite in the opposite wing to the family; he took the steps up two at a time, eager to get the conversation over with. When he entered the bedroom, however, he found Cressida asleep on the bed. He stood in the doorway for a long while, not wanting to wake her. There was a tightness in his chest that he couldn't understand.

He had no way to be sure what she would decide once he told her of the option to annul their short marriage. He could simply make a phone call and have parliament vote against the whole thing, bury the entire idea as though it had never existed. She would never even know it had been spoken of...

But that would be selfish and he had gained enough self-awareness to know that he could not make this kind of choice for her. Lying to her or withholding information was not protecting her, it was something the old Khal would have done from a place of fear. Regressing was not something that he could justify. She had not been shown much kindness in her life, despite her royal upbringing. She had been used as a pawn in battles between her parents and palmed off as a political sacrifice to a man who was far too broken to ever give her the kind of life she deserved. She deserved to live the life she chose, even if that life did not include him.

Cressida stirred in the bed, a smile brightening her entire face at the same moment that she opened her eyes and saw him. 'What time is it?' she murmured huskily, stretching her arms.

'Almost six,' Khal said, forcing himself to remain still when all he wanted to do was close the distance between them and draw her into his embrace.

'Did the meeting go well? Have you come to an agreement for the press strategy?' she asked, standing up to reveal she wore only one of his T-shirts. She smirked as his gaze darkened. 'Sorry, I couldn't bear the thought of digging through half of the gowns in my case to find my own T-shirt so I stole one of yours.'

This image might very well be imprinted on his brain for ever, he thought with a cruel twist of his lips. She had never looked more tempting than at this moment, wearing one of his white T-shirts. The garment went to her mid-thigh, showcasing her long slim legs. But he was not a barbarian, even though the world claimed he was. Putting his libido firmly in check, he took a few steps away, just as they were interrupted by her assistants arriving to begin preparing her for the evening.

Cressida looked at him uncertainly. 'Is everything all right?' she asked with a frown. 'I can have them come back if you need to talk?'

Khal paused, realising that he had just been about to launch into a very heavy conversation less than an hour before they were due to be seen in public. Cursing his own stupidity, he hastily assured her that everything was okay and excused himself to allow her team to go about their preparations. There was plenty of time to talk tomorrow, he told himself. One more night would not change matters. He went about readying himself, ignoring the niggling feeling that he was simply delaying the inevitable.

Cressida moved to the edge of the party; the air had become uncomfortably warm as more and more guests arrived. She had been told there would be a small gathering of Monteverrian dignitaries and wealthy society favourites in order to show that the royal family stood strong against the scandal. But it seemed half of the kingdom had arrived to get a glimpse of the Sheikh of Zayyar and his scandalous wife.

But as she breathed in the night air, looking at the beautiful ornate fountain and surrounding shrubbery, all lit up in pink and orange lights, she wondered if a husband who was simply understanding would ever be enough. Her mother had said that she and her father had experienced a burning passion in the beginning, then that passion had burnt out, leaving nothing but discontent and resentment in its wake. Without a true emotional connection, would she ever feel secure in her marriage?

'It seems desert life suits you,' a familiar voice came from behind her. Cressida turned to find her middle sister, Olivia, standing in the doorway, her silver gown sparkling like an angel. She couldn't help it; she burst into tears just as Olivia's arms surrounded her in an embrace.

'What are you doing here?' she half choked between sobs.

Olivia wiped one of the tears from her cheek, her classically beautiful features filled with concern. 'We saw the news and we came straight here. Did you know about…the affair?'

Cressida filled her sister in on the entire story, beginning with her mother's version of the affair, leading into her own discovery and Fabian's subsequent emotional blackmail. Once she had finished, they sat in silence for a moment, Olivia shaking her head slightly.

'This family is utterly insane,' Olivia said simply. 'I have never been more grateful for my new distance.'

Cressida smiled, leaning her head against her sister's arm for a moment. Olivia had been the only person she had ever felt a true connection with in her family. Eleanor had always been too busy to entertain her, being the oldest and set to become Queen of Monteverre one day. But Olivia had taught her how to braid her hair and told her the latest gossip from school. She had always envied her sister for her natural beauty and easy elegance. She was talented too, having recently taken the reins of their grandmother's literacy foundation after relinquishing her royal status.

'You seem happy,' Cressida said. 'I'm glad.'

'Roman is wonderful,' Olivia said, a dreamy look crossing her features. 'But I'm also feeling fulfilment from working for the first time in my life.' She smiled widely. 'But I'm sure you know all about that, having had years of freedom in London.'

Cressida thought of that time in her life; it seemed so long ago. 'I do miss it,' she said truthfully. 'I envy you.'

'You could always join forces with me; goodness knows I could use someone with your kind of language skills, Cress.' Olivia's eyes lit up for a moment before she frowned. 'But, of course, you have your own set of responsibilities now. I doubt the Sheikha of a country has time to go travelling around the world teaching children to read?'

The sudden mixture of longing and disappointment that filled her chest took her by surprise. The idea of travelling, seeing the world while at the same time using her knowledge and expertise to teach... She sighed wistfully. But, of course, she had her life in Zayyar and her duties as Sheikha. That should be enough for her. She loved Khal and a small part of her hoped that in time he could come to love her too. But the thought of teaching...

Olivia cleared her throat beside her. 'We could join

forces to do a one off event with the foundation, maybe. It would be great to reconnect and spend time together.'

Cressida opened her mouth to speak, but at the same moment Khal decided to make his appearance on the terrace, followed closely by Roman Lazarov. Olivia's Russian fiancé had once been Khal's Chief of Security and best friend. It wasn't exactly clear how he had come to be engaged to her sister, but it was obvious that it had made things strained between the two men. Khal looked from Cressida to her sister, an unreadable expression crossing his features.

'Olivia was just telling me about her work with the literacy foundation,' Cressida said brightly, covertly trying to swipe away the remnants of her crying episode from her cheeks.

'It's nice to see you again, Sheikh Khalil.' Olivia smiled, nodding politely. 'I was just trying to persuade my sister to put her amazing language skills to good use with the literacy foundation.'

A strange expression crossed Khal's dark features as he looked from Olivia to her. 'Cressida is very talented. She would make an excellent teacher.'

Cressida blushed. She had expected to feel some jealousy with Olivia, considering that her sister had been Khal's original intended bride. But for some reason she did not. Maybe it was the way that Roman and her sister looked at each other, so full of love and happiness. Or maybe it was the fact that she still held out hope that Khal might come to look at her in that same way.

A commotion inside the doorway took their attention and Khal moved aside just in time for the terrace doors to swing open and Queen Aurelia to burst through them.

'I'm done! I want divorce papers drawn up immediately in the morning,' the older woman proclaimed, followed closely by Eleanor and King Fabian. A trio of guards closed the terrace doors, blocking out the scene from the rest of the party.

'Mother, please. At least wait until tomorrow,' Eleanor chided in her best peacekeeping voice as she took her mother by the hand.

'I've waited decades!' Aurelia exclaimed.

Cressida was shocked to realise that her mother was sober; she could tell by the lucidity in her eyes and the hint of colour in her cheeks. She could not remember the last time she had seen her mother look so awake and present.

'Another grand debacle for the entire society to talk about,' King Fabian said, bored. 'I suppose it has been a few months since the last embarrassment.' He looked pointedly towards Roman and Olivia.

Khal moved to Cressida's side, taking her by the hand. 'I think it's best if we go back inside,' he said quietly.

'And leave them like this?'

'They are adults, *habibti*. There is nothing we can do to change whatever is about to transpire. You will only put yourself in the firing line by being present.'

Cressida nodded at his sense, feeling a glow of warmth in the way he stood as her protector. She made to move with him towards the doors, whispering a quiet goodbye to her sisters as her mother continued to berate her father loudly in the background.

'Hold on just a moment,' King Fabian cut across his wife's emotional tirade, his eyes black slits as he took a step towards Cressida. 'As I'm apparently about to suffer an embarrassing and probably expensive divorce, can I at least take it that you two lovebirds have decided to remain married after all?'

Cressida frowned at her father's question—what did he mean, *remain married*? She looked up at Khal, seeing that same stressed expression that he had been wearing all evening.

'This is not the time or the place, Fabian,' Khal gritted.

'I want it in writing that you will not nullify the marriage or the financial transactions that came with it, do you hear me? I want it iron-clad or I will make sure that your kingdom suffers every political roadblock possible.'

'What is he talking about?' Cressida turned to her husband.

'We will speak in private,' Khal gritted, his attention still focused on her father. There was a dangerous glint in his eyes, an awful ruthlessness that she had never witnessed before. It made her recoil slightly, taking a step back from him.

'Cressida,' he said sternly, 'I will not discuss this here.' He reached for her but was blocked by her two sisters, who moved in to stand at her sides.

'What is he talking about…a nullification?' Cressida asked, feeling her hands begin to tremble.

'Parliament have undertaken a motion to dismiss our marriage contract on the grounds of forgery.' Khal's voice was emotionless as he spoke. 'They are saying that because you deliberately withheld the truth of your parentage that I can choose to nullify the contract.'

Cressida felt the ground sway beneath her. 'I see.'

'I did not wish to discuss this with an audience.' He met her eyes. 'I think this is a matter that we should weigh up alone.'

Weigh up? He was discussing the possibility of ending their marriage as though the list of pros and cons was endless. Cressida thought that if she could actually feel her own heart breaking, the pain would be unbearable. As it was, she simply felt numb. 'I don't think we need to weigh up much. If parliament says that my parentage is unacceptable then you need to do what is right for your kingdom. I won't contest any nullification.'

Cressida moved past her sisters and went through the terrace doors, needing to be alone before she let herself completely fall to pieces. She heard the commotion behind her but refused to look back, asking a guard to escort her to her suite. She heard footsteps thundering up the stairs behind them but ignored them, hoping her guard would do his job. Apparently the Zayyari guards only served one ruler, she thought wryly as Khal came striding in the door, slightly out of breath from his sprint.

Khal was silent for a long moment. 'You won't contest it…or you are relieved that it is a possibility?'

'I think if either of us is relieved, it's you. I am hardly the golden bride with political influence that you hoped for. I am steeped in scandal, for goodness' sake. I can hardly make a speech without stuttering.' She shook her head wildly. 'I'm not my sister, Khal. I have tried to measure up as her replacement but I simply can't. Maybe this is best for both of us, to end this now before we go any deeper.'

'How much deeper can we get?' he said, exasperated. 'I know that this marriage did not start out in the most conventional way. I may have chosen your sister first out of convenience, Cressida, but I did not even know that you existed at that time.'

'So if you knew about me, if you could go back and make the choice again, you'd choose me? The awkward, nerdy, antisocial anti-Princess?' she said in complete disbelief.

'I cannot promise that I would have chosen you, given my decision to enter into a loveless marriage. All I cared about was that my bride met criteria.' He moved closer. 'But I would never change you, now that I know the real you. Now that we have begun to share our lives.'

Cressida felt her breath catch in her throat at his words. Surely he didn't mean that he didn't want the annulment? Suddenly she wasn't quite sure exactly who was arguing for or against their marriage any more.

He ran a hand across his jaw, shaking his head. 'What I am offering you now is a real life time machine. A chance to change your future if you want it. Your sister has already offered you a teaching position. If you tell me that you want our marriage annulled, I will honour your request. My conscience would not allow me to hide this from you, much as I may have wanted to.'

'You considered not telling me?'

'God, yes. Why on earth would I want to give you a failsafe chance to walk away from this marriage? Away from me?'

'I just presumed…your plans to have the perfect Sheikha have all gone up in smoke. I'm a walking scandal. Why on earth would you stay weighed down by the burden of me?'

He paused for a moment, the air between them frozen in time. Her heartbeat seemed uncomfortably loud in the silent room and she wondered if he could hear it.

'Yes, you may be a walking scandal. And your family may be utterly insane, and your personality may be better suited to the position of librarian rather than Sheikha…but I promise you, after we have grown closer these past weeks, that you are the woman I would choose over and over again.'

She forgot to breathe, hardly believing what she had just heard. As she watched, he moved closer, coming down on one knee in front of her.

'Cressida… If you truly want to end this marriage, I promise that I will not force you to stay. I have spent so long trying to control everyone and everything around me. Trying to find some sort of peace within myself.' He took her hand, his eyes never leaving hers. 'But I cannot promise that I won't spend every day finding new ways to beg you to come back to me for the rest of my life.'

'Why would you do that?' she breathed.

'Because, while I may have been too afraid to realise my feelings for you before, I know them now. I will not give up on fighting to win your heart. I was afraid to let you all the way in, for fear I would need you too much. It seems laughable now, really, trying to resist my own destiny.'

'You said you don't believe in fate or soulmates.' She felt her insides shake at the look in his eyes, at the sensation that the ground might fall away from under her at any moment.

'Is it not more than coincidence that in a club full of people, in a city with a population twice the size of my entire kingdom…that you would choose me?'

He took a deep breath. 'I realised something today. From the moment I held you in my arms on that dance floor the first night we met, I felt peace. That was what I was running from. I had been so used to feeling at war within myself that feeling your warmth calming me was terrifying. It was as though you took a grip of the darkness in my soul and forced me out into the light again. If that is not love, I don't know what is.'

'I don't know what to say,' Cressida breathed, feeling her hands tremble as he raised one to his lips.

'Say that you will stay by my side. Not just as my Sheikha and my wife, but as my true partner in life. My love.'

It was the romantic proposal she had never received, she realised. She pressed her lips together to stop them from trembling.

'Nothing would make me happier than to stay by your side.' She lowered herself to her knees in front of him, placing one hand on his cheek. 'But I need to be true to myself as well as to my love for you.'

He frowned but she continued quickly, 'I cannot just be a silent figure in a pretty dress by your side. I want to use my skills to help people, to do good in the world.'

A slow smile lit up the darkness in his eyes. 'I will support you in whatever you wish to do with that wonderful brain of yours. You may count on me to stand silently by your side and look pretty in the process.'

She felt the last shred of resistance melt away as she leaned in and pressed her lips to his. He responded by pulling her deep into the circle of his arms, surrounding her with his strength. She felt it in his kiss, the raw power of his love for her. She had not known that this was the missing piece of her heart until he had come into her life and showed her what it meant to be supported and loved for who she was. That she was enough. For Cressida, there could be no greater gift.

EPILOGUE

Six months later...

THE PARISIAN HOTEL ballroom was full to bursting with members of royalty and celebrities alike. Everyone had joined to celebrate the wedding of the year with the most scandalous royal family of the decade. Cressida watched as her sister walked onto the dance floor, accompanied by her handsome new husband for their first dance. 'Olivia looks so happy,' she murmured.

'Roman was never much of a dancer; it appears he has taken lessons.' Khal laughed.

'I will never understand the relationship you two have.' Cressida raised one brow.

'Nor would I expect you to.' He smiled. 'We are both as complicated as each other, but underneath we will always be friends. Brothers now, I suppose.'

'A strange family set-up, if ever I knew one.' She laughed huskily in her throat, gasping as she felt Khal lean in and lay a kiss on the nape of her neck.

'The party is practically over now; surely we can slip away unnoticed?' he murmured playfully, his teeth nipping the side of her ear.

'I am not going anywhere alone with you, Your Highness, not after how little sleep I got last night with you sharing my bed once more.'

Khal had been away for a week while he launched the grand tourism season in the now thriving city of Valar. She had been forced to return early from a trip to South America with the literacy foundation and remain on bed rest at the palace for reasons that they could not yet disclose to the public.

'I hope I did not truly exhaust you?' Genuine concern filled his features as he turned her to look at him. 'You know the doctor said that you needed to rest as much as possible for a couple of weeks.'

Cressida found herself laying one hand across the gentle swell of her stomach in an unconscious show of maternal protection. 'The intense sickness has seemed to ease now that we have got through the first few months. I heard the first trimester is the most difficult.'

Khal nodded, a tight smile crossing his features. His change of heart regarding a family of their own had come as an enormous surprise to Cressida. She had fully intended to respect Khal's wishes to remain without natural heirs, despite knowing that deep down she longed to become a mother some day. But as he had relaxed into the ease of their relationship, she had noticed he tended to worry less and less about things he could not control.

It was not effortless for him. He was a natural protector, after all. It seemed his urge to protect those he loved also included a wish to have children of his own. She had been only too happy to fulfil her wifely duties in that regard, rejoicing when she had fallen pregnant almost immediately. She had not told either of her sisters yet, especially knowing that Olivia's wedding was so close. She did not want to detract from the day.

But as she watched the newlywed couple slow dance

together, she thought she could see a similar glow in her sister's cheeks as Roman's hand slid covertly to her stomach for the briefest of moments. Her eyes met Olivia's across the crowded ballroom, her sister's answering smile telling her all that she needed to know.

'Are you nervous?' Cressida asked a while later as she lay cradled in her husband's arms in the master bedroom of their hotel suite. 'For the baby, I mean.'

Khal moved his powerful body behind her, holding her tight to his chest as he drew lazy circles on her abdomen with one finger. 'Of course I'm nervous. But I think most people are, even if they have not been through a loss. My biggest concern is fighting the urge to place you on permanent bed rest and lock you away for the next six months.'

'Six months in bed?' Cressida pretended to seriously consider that scenario. 'Would you be there too?'

'These hormones have turned you into a sex-crazed hellion,' he scolded, flipping on top of her. 'We have already made love twice today and you still have energy.'

Cressida felt a moment of complete happiness wash over her, looking up into the eyes of the man who loved her. It was almost overwhelming.

'What is it?' Khal asked, a furrow forming in his brow as Cressida's eyes welled up with unshed tears.

'I just realised… I have spent my whole life wanting more and feeling like I would never deserve it. And now here I am with everything that I will ever want or need right here in this bed. I never have to feel alone again.'

'Never,' Khal murmured against her lips, drawing her into his embrace. 'As long as you want me I am yours.'

* * * * *

COMING SOON!

We really hope you enjoyed reading this book. If you're looking for more romance, be sure to head to the shops when new books are available on

Thursday 27th June

To see which titles are coming soon, please visit
millsandboon.co.uk/nextmonth

MILLS & BOON

Coming next month

DEMANDING HIS HIDDEN HEIR
Jackie Ashenden

'*Buono notte,* Mrs St George,' Enzo said in that deep voice she
knew so well, the one that had once been full of heat and yet now
was so cold. 'I think you and I need to have a little chat.'

'A chat?' she said huskily, her chin firming, the shock and fear
in her gaze quickly masked. 'A chat about what?'

With an effort, Enzo dragged his gaze from her throat.

So, she was going to pretend she didn't know what he was talking
about, was she? Well, unfortunately for her, he wasn't having it.

'I'm not here to play games with you, Summer,' he said coldly.
'Or should I say *Matilda.* I'm here to talk about my son.'

Another burst of quicksilver emotion flashed in her eyes, then
it was gone, nothing but a cool wall of grey in its place. 'Yes,
that's my name. You don't have to say it like a pantomime villain.
And as to a son…Well.' Her chin came up. 'I don't know what
you're talking about.'

'Is that how you're going to play this?' He didn't bother to temper
the acid in his tone. 'You're going to pretend you don't know anything
about that child you just rescued downstairs? The child with eyes
the same colour as mine?' He took a step towards her. 'Perhaps
you're going to pretend that you don't know who I am either.'

She held her ground, even though she didn't have anywhere
to go, not when there was a wall behind her. 'No, of course not.'
Her gaze didn't flicker. 'I know who you are, Enzo Cardinali.'

The sound of his name in her soft, husky voice made a bolt
of lightning shoot straight down his spine, helplessly reminding
him of other times when she'd said it.

'Good.' He kept his voice hard, trying not to let the heat creep
into it. 'Then if you know who I am you can explain to me why
you didn't tell me that I have a son.'

She was already pale; now she went the colour of ashes. But

that defiant slant to her chin remained, the expression in her eyes guarded. 'Like I said, I don't know what you're talking about.'

Enzo's rage, already inflamed by his body's betrayal, curdled into something very close to incandescence and it burned like fire in his blood, thick and hot.

He'd never been so angry in all his life, some distant part of him vaguely appalled at the intensity of his emotions—a reminder that he needed to lock it down, since his iron control was the only thing that set him apart from his power-hungry father.

But in this moment he didn't care.

This woman, this beautiful, sexy, infuriating woman, hadn't told him he had a son and, more, she'd kept it from him for four years.

Four. Years.

He took another step towards her, unable to help himself, the heat in his veins so hot it felt as if it was going to ignite him where he stood. 'I see. So you *are* going to pretend you know nothing. How depressingly predictable of you.'

'Simon is *my* son.' Her hands had gone into fists at her sides and she didn't move, not an inch. 'And H-Henry's.' Her gaze was as cool as winter rain, but that slight stutter gave her away.

'No.' Enzo kept his voice honed as a steel blade. 'He is not. Those eyes are singular to the Cardinali line. Which makes him mine.'

'But I—'

'How long have you known, *Matilda*? A year? Two?' He took another step, forcing her back against the wall.

Enzo put a hand on the wall at one side of her silky red head and leaned in close so she had no choice but to stare straight at him. 'Look at me, *cara*. Look at me and tell me that you don't see your son staring back.'

Continue reading
DEMANDING HIS HIDDEN HEIR
Jackie Ashenden

Available next month
www.millsandboon.co.uk

LET'S TALK
Romance

For exclusive extracts, competitions
and special offers, find us online:

For all the latest titles coming soon, visit
millsandboon.co.uk/nextmonth